Birdwatcher's Quarry

Alan Power, British intelligence agent and friend of Tommy Hambledon, had come down to the little French village of Arnage-sur-Loire on the trail of something big. Tommy had given Power two assistants, agents Campbell and Forgan, and his blessing; the next thing Tommy heard of Power was the news of his death in a motor accident . . . an "accident" to which Campbell and Forgan had been witnesses.

It didn't take long to determine that Power had been shot in the head while driving his racing car around a dangerous curve. And it wasn't long before still another witness declared himself: an elderly ornithologist who rapidly became a figure of mystery.

Tommy Hambledon is at his inimitable best in this absorbing tale, unswerving in his search for a friend's killer despite the amusing eccentricities of Forgan and Campbell and despite a unique threat—a threat not only to his life but to his bachelorhood.

Scene: France

This novel has not appeared in any form prior to book publication.

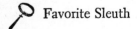 Favorite Sleuth

BY MANNING COLES

Novels:

THE FAR TRAVELLER

HAPPY RETURNS

BRIEF CANDLES

THIS FORTRESS

Intrigue and Adventure:

BIRDWATCHER'S QUARRY

THE BASLE EXPRESS

THE MAN IN THE GREEN HAT

ALL THAT GLITTERS

ALIAS UNCLE HUGO

NIGHT TRAIN TO PARIS

NOW OR NEVER

DANGEROUS BY NATURE

DIAMONDS TO AMSTERDAM

NOT NEGOTIABLE

AMONG THOSE ABSENT

LET THE TIGER DIE

WITH INTENT TO DECEIVE

THE FIFTH MAN

GREEN HAZARD

WITHOUT LAWFUL AUTHORITY

THEY TELL NO TALES

TOAST TO TOMORROW

DRINK TO YESTERDAY

Books for Boys:

GREAT CAESAR'S GHOST

MANNING COLES

Birdwatcher's Quarry

PUBLISHED FOR THE CRIME CLUB BY
Doubleday & Company, Inc.
Garden City, New York, 1956

*All of the characters in this book are fictitious
and any resemblance to actual persons,
living or dead, is purely coincidental.*

Contents

CAST

Thomas Elphinstone Hambledon

Alexander Campbell ⎤
Manuel Carboni ⎦

William Forgan ⎤
Benito Farelli ⎦

Alan Power, of M. I. 5

Dr. Alexandre Evette

Police Constable Jean Maroche, of Arnage-sur-Loire

Vidal, detective sergeant, of the Orleans police

M. Jules Barbeau, farmer, of Arnage-sur-Loire

Gallet, undermanager of the Hotel de la Poste

Raoul Rougisson, an ornithologist

Pierre Lacroix, manager of the Hotel de la Poste

Peyret, journalist, of the *Orleans Intelligencer*

Polydore d'Aquitaine, a tramp

Marius Aldebert, a financier, and *Julius*, his brother

Jean Jaboulet, called the Spider, a private enquiry agent

Antoine Letord, Chief Superintendent of the Sûreté

The Señores Buonaventure and Goyaz, from Campos de Oro

Madame Tiffet, proprietress of the Café de Bruges

Alphonse, a Rhode Island Red cock

Madeleine, a chinchilla rabbit

Police, hotel servants, small boys, etc.

SCENES: The village of Arnage-sur-Loire and Paris

TIME: The present day

CHAPTER 1   *The Poor Monsieur*

DR. BENITO FARELLI and his patient, Señor Manuelo Carboni, sat side by side on the short turf in the sunshine and admired the view, which was, indeed, worth admiring since they were looking down upon a stretch of the Loire. The hillside upon which they sat dropped away below them, and across it, like a shelf, there ran a country road edged for the most part with bushes, though just below where the men were sitting it was open to view. Below the road the ground fell away very steeply before flattening out into the meadows which bordered the Loire; just at the point where the drop was most steep the road took a sharp bend to follow the contour of the hill. The result was a very nasty corner indeed, and such traffic as was accustomed to use the road approached it with the respect it deserved. Otherwise the scene was innocent, harmless, and soothing to the nerves upon a fine morning in May; possibly this was the reason why the two men were sitting there placidly enjoying the sunshine, for the Señor Médico Farelli was understood in the village to be a brilliantly clever psychiatrist, the pride of his Faculty in Madrid, and his patient was a rich orange grower who was recovering from a nervous breakdown brought on, it was said, by overwork.

As part of the cure, they were travelling about Europe in a large antique Rolls driven by an English chauffeur; they had taken rooms at the Hotel de la Poste at Arnage-sur-Loire for a few days because they had taken a liking to it. They said so to the hotel undermanager, who had demurred when he found that one of his guests was a little eccentric.

"Not," he explained, "that I should ever wish to be discourteous or unhelpful towards a poor gentleman who has been ill, but I must consider my other guests."

"I reassure you completely," said Dr. Farelli. "My patient is entirely harmless. Amiable. Charming. Docile. In short, lovable."

"No doubt. But——"

"He makes great strides towards recovery; would you have it on your conscience that——"

"No, no. But there are other villages where the air is equally pure and invigorating."

"Doubtless. But not in every village is there such a total absence of fruiterers' shops. I will let you into a secret. The only thing which now disturbs my convalescent is the sight of oranges. He associates them, you understand, with his unfortunate neurosis."

"But how to ensure—does he become violent?"

"Never," said the doctor earnestly, "and never did. He only dances."

"Dances. Dances?"

"Only at the sight of oranges, especially in neat piles. I repeat, he is all but cured; he used to dance at the sight of lemons and also coconuts. But, I assure you, never apples or pears. Never."

The undermanager considered the matter and then shook his head.

"I could not risk it, monsieur. There might one day be oranges in the dining-room——"

"But we should, naturally, dine in our own room. You have a private salon at our disposal?"

This was different, naturally. Guests who demanded accommodation upon this scale were not lightly to be brushed off. There was that suite which could so seldom be let *en bloc.*

"I have a suite——" began the undermanager.

The travellers had been at Arnage for just over a week and no one had been so tactless as to produce oranges.

They sat on their hillside, smoking companionably and not talking much until their attention was drawn to the road by a lorry labouring up the gradient from their right with its engine spluttering and backfiring. There was also a car coming down the hill from the left a small sports car painted scarlet; the top was folded down and even the windshield lay flat upon the hood. The driver was a young man whose fair hair swirled about his head with the wind of his passage.

"Dear me," said Farelli, "here comes Power. I thought he was starting an hour ago."

"So did I," said Carboni. "Driving even faster than usual, the idiot. He'll kill himself one of these days."

"I suppose he's trying to make up time, but he must slow down for that corner."

The roar of the high-speed engine came up to their ears and changed its note as the driver lifted his foot. The car was lost to sight for a moment behind a screen of bushes and reappeared again exactly upon the corner. As it did so, the watchers saw the driver fall over sideways in his seat; his hands dropped from the wheel and the car failed to take the bend. It went straight on, checked for an instant on the edge as the front wheels dropped and then slid over with a grinding noise and a series of horrible crashing sounds, out of sight into the valley below.

The lorry driver, who was by this time only twenty yards short of the corner himself, uttered a yell of horror, pulled his vehicle into the side of the road, and leapt out of the cab. Farelli and Carboni sprang to their feet and rushed down to the road, then all three together slipped and scrambled down the steep slope to where the car lay with its wheels in the air and still slowly turning; before the men reached it a flicker of flame leapt into a flare and a column of black smoke rose up and leaned against the hillside.

The driver's body had been thrown clear, but it was obvious at a glance that he was very dead. The lorry driver removed his beret and the Spaniards took off their hats.

"Did you see that?" stammered the driver, "did you also see it? *Sainte Vierge*, it was the steering—the poor young man—never shall I forget——"

"He is dead," said the temperamental Señor Carboni rapidly, "he is dead, he is dead. How dead he is, is he not? All broken up." He uttered a loud discordant laugh and began to shake all over, his long legs—for he was a tall lean man—wobbling so that his knees went in and out, his arms shaking loosely from the shoulders and his head rolling upon his thin neck. "He is dead, is he not dead? Yes."

"Calm yourself," said his medical adviser, laying a hand on his arm. "Calm yourself. The young man is now in Paradise. My friend," to the lorry driver, "this is a matter for the police. Will you remain here while I go to summon them?"

"No, I'll go," said the driver, showing the whites of his eyes and backing away from Carboni, "I'll go. I can go in the lorry quicker. What's the matter with him?" he added in a whisper. "Loony?"

"A little nervous, that is all," said Farelli reassuringly, but Carboni was standing upon one leg, winding the other round it and writhing his arms together above his head. The driver did not like it.

"Dear Heaven, he's turning himself into a tree," he said. "I'm off. I'll tell the police. Good-bye." He made a run at the hillside and almost at once disappeared into the smoke. It was not, however, until explosive noises from the road above proclaimed the lorry to be on its way that Señor Carboni unwound himself and joined Farelli, who was bending over the body.

"What I want to know," said Farelli, "is why he fell over sideways like that. I mean, why fall sideways?"

"Seizure of some kind?" suggested Carboni. "Heart attack?"

"He'd fall back, or forwards on the wheel. He might roll sideways after that, but not as he did. You saw it too, didn't you?"

Carboni nodded. "Anyone would think he'd been hit. Small boy with catapult?"

"Come and hold his head. Oh lord, how excessively nasty. However, truth must be served, or so they say, though I've often wondered why. What thick hair he's got."

"Is your truth really necessary—what have you got there?"

"A bullet hole," said Farelli soberly.

A quarter of an hour later the village doctor drove up in his old clover-leaf Citroën with the local police constable sitting beside him. Since the smoke was still crawling up the hillside and obscuring the road, they pulled up just short of the corner where Power had gone off the road. They walked on, noticing the marks on the grass edge where the car had gone over; when they had passed through the drift of smoke they came upon the two Spaniards. Dr. Farelli, still with his hat in his hand, was standing on the verge looking mournfully down upon the huddle of brown tweed below which was the body of Alan Power. Carboni was working along the hillside just above the road, picking a bunch of wild flowers.

Farelli looked round at the sound of footsteps.

"Good morning, Dr. Evette," he said in a subdued voice. "A melancholy occasion. Good morning, Maroche."

The village doctor was an old man who had lived in Arnage for over forty years; he had a bristling grey beard and pale grey eyes behind strong glasses. He nodded to Farelli, whom he knew slightly, and also looked over the brink.

"I assume that the man is dead," he said.

"Completely," said Farelli.

"He looks it," said Evette, and began to sidle carefully down the steep slope.

"The lorry driver," said Police Constable Maroche, "stated that you, monsieur, also saw the accident. Is that true?"

"Perfectly true," said Farelli. "The poor man came along the road from that direction, travelling, in my opinion, much too fast."

"Did he not, then, slow down for the corner?"

"Not enough, it seems. I heard the note of the engine change. I could not see him at that point. I and my patient, the Señor Carboni here, you know him"—the policeman nodded sympathetically—"were sitting on the grass just up there. The car appeared at the corner but could not turn it. It went straight on and——" Farelli threw up his hands.

"Deplorable," said Maroche. "Monsieur will be required to give his evidence."

"Naturally," said Farelli. "Of course. But not, I trust, my patient."

"It will not, I imagine, be necessary to trouble the poor Monsieur Carboni."

"I am greatly obliged to you for your courteous consideration."

"It is nothing, monsieur."

"May we, then, return to our hotel? We have had," said Farelli with a sweet, sad smile, "an unhappily agitating morning."

"It is understood, monsieur. Au revoir," said Maroche, saluting.

Carboni galloped up with a bouquet, composed mainly of dandelions, which he handed to the constable.

"Give him, please, these poor flowers from me. Tell him I am very sorry that he is dead."

"Willingly, monsieur," said the constable, rising to the occasion. Farelli gave him an understanding smile and took Carboni by the arm. Together they wandered vaguely up the road while Maroche plunged down the hillside. The moment he was well out of sight the two Spaniards quickened their pace and hurried back to where the doctor had left his car.

"It must have been just about here," said Carboni, "that Power was shot. It would be short of the corner, or the car wouldn't have gone straight on."

Farelli agreed and pulled a thin and reasonably straight switch out of the hedge. "This car is higher than his, but it's near enough. Will you sit in the driving seat for a moment? The entry hole was just above the ear."

He held the switch up in approximately the probable line of the bullet, and Carboni twisted his head to look along it.

"Among these bushes somewhere," he said. "It would be, of course, and from a point where he had a clear view. Come on."

The place was not difficult to find; there were not many spots which gave a clear view of any length of the road. When they found it there was a plain impression in the grass to show where someone had been sitting and a couple of cigarette stubs to show that he had passed some time in waiting. Carboni picked them up.

"Gauloise Bleue," he said. "So helpful," for this cigarette is the woodbine of France. He cast about, picked up a forked stick, and showed Farelli the damp earth still coating six inches of the longest end. "Gun rest."

Farelli grunted and hunted about in the thin grass until, with another grunt, he picked up what he had been looking for, an ejected cartridge case.

"Point two-two."

"You didn't tell the policeman about the bullet hole?"

"No," said Farelli. "I thought that they'd like to find that for themselves, if they do. I assume there'll be an autopsy."

"If I were handed a corpse as comprehensively smashed up as that one, it wouldn't occur to me to look for a bullet hole as well," said Carboni pensively. "One must be fair. Did you hear a shot fired?"

"No, did you? How could one, with the roar of Power's super-charged effort and the lorry making noises like the Battle of the Boyne? Let's go back to the hotel; we'd better not be seen poking about."

"We'll have the Rolls out this afternoon and have a quiet drive to calm my mind. We'll go somewhere about twenty miles off and make a nice long telephone call. After all, we are not here merely to enjoy ourselves. Come on."

Thomas Elphinstone Hambledon took the telephone call in his own room at MI 5, thought over the news it contained for as long as it takes to smoke a cigarette, and then went along the passage to see his immediate superior.

"That young Alan Power," he began. "I've just had a telephone message to say he's dead."

"Dead? What, in an accident?"

"It looked like that," said Tommy accurately. "He failed to take a bend and the car went over a cliff."

"I am not altogether surprised," said the other, "if he was driving that red MG of his. He was a bit of a demon. But I'm sorry to hear it, all the same; he was quite good and steadily getting better. Besides, I liked him. What a stupid waste of a good life, to die in a road accident. Of course we——"

"I said it looked like an accident."

"Eh?"

"In point of fact, he had a bullet in the head. It's true it was only a point two-two, so it may not have killed him outright, but it's enough to account for his having failed to take the bend. The entry hole was about an inch above the right ear, I am told."

"I see. Well now, suppose you tell me the rest. Come clean, Hambledon. Who rang you up?"

"I don't know a great deal myself. Power came over to see me about a fortnight—more than that, three weeks ago—mainly about that job in Paris which is practically cleaned up, and he said he had dropped by accident on the traces of something so big that personally he didn't believe it, but it might be true all the same. I asked him what it was and he wouldn't tell me. He said he was a rising—he hoped—intelligence man and not just telling bedtime stories. Not that this, if true, was much of a bedtime story. I told him to come off it, but he refused. He was not, he said, reporting it officially as it might well be a plate of duck soup and he didn't want to be laughed at, but he would rather like a couple of intelligent helpers. So, since he steadfastly refused to have anyone from the department, I took him down the Clerkenwell Road and introduced him to Campbell and Forgan. I mean, they are not on the establishment."

"Those two fellows who keep a model shop. I've never met them, as it happens, but I've heard stories. You've told me some. They've done several jobs with you at various times, I know."

"Yes," said Hambledon. "Well, I gather that they packed up and went, because I got a picture postcard from Bordeaux, but nothing after that until today. They are staying at a place called Arnage-sur-Loire, and that's where the accident happened. Alleged accident."

"I suppose the French police are enquiring into the shooting business."

"If they know about it." Hambledon gave a summary of the story. "The French doctor won't be looking for a bullet hole. Why should he? On the other hand, Forgan and Campbell were not the only witnesses; there was also a lorry driver. If he says that Power suddenly fell sideways, the French may wonder why and subsequently find out. Our men said they'd held their tongues because they didn't know what we should want to do about it."

"I think you had better go out there yourself, Hambledon. There's not only poor Power, there's also whatever he thought he'd found. Perhaps your model-makers know something about it."

"I hope so," said Hambledon earnestly.

CHAPTER 2   *Official Enquiry*

WHEN THERE is a fatal road accident in France
there is no inquest as the English know it. The police make enquiries both of eyewitnesses and of anyone else who may have
useful information to give. After that there is an official enquiry
by a Juge d'Instruction to discover who was responsible for the
accident and to take proceedings against him.

If no one is to blame except the driver and he is dead, the
second half of the programme is, naturally, not carried out. It
is an obvious waste of time to spend even half a day trying and
convicting one who has already passed beyond the reach of justice.

In Power's case, therefore, the Gendarmerie thought that they
had only to take statements from the two eyewitnesses, Dr. Farelli
and the lorry driver. One would not, naturally, pester *ce pauvre
monsieur* the Señor Carboni; besides, it would be useless. After
that a report would be made out for the files, a certificate issued
to authorize burial, and the affair would be finished.

They took these statements accordingly, and though they were
not on oath both Farelli and the lorry driver told the exact truth
of what they had seen. Both said that Power rolled over sideways in his seat, but no one seemed to think that there was anything notable about this. Dr. Evette of Arnage-sur-Loire, who
examined the body, testified that the poor young man had died
of shock from multiple injuries, being indeed so comprehensively
broken up that it would be impossible to say that this or that killed
him first. The constable gave his report upon what he found at
the scene of the crash, and the picture appeared to be unmis-
takably clear.

"Deplorable," said the uniformed Inspector from Orleans who
was in charge of the enquiry, "deplorable but quite simple. If

these young men will drive like that upon such a road—— I will sign the certificate, but the body had better remain in the mortuary here until instructions for its disposal have been received from England. No doubt he has relatives. We are communicating with the address on his passport. Let everything be done decently. He was not without money, this young man. There is nothing else here today? Then I go back to Orleans, for there is plenty there for me. Au 'voir. He got into his car and drove away.

"I suppose," said Farelli to Carboni, "I suppose we did right to keep quiet about the bullet hole?"

"I suppose so. Hambledon will be here in the morning; he can take over. Find the bullet hole for himself, or something. Or keep it quiet altogether, why not?"

Next morning the village was all agog with the news that the mortuary had been broken into during the night. Power's body, not yet coffined, lay on the slab covered with a sheet; the clothes he had been wearing had been brushed and cleaned and were tidily folded upon a table at one side. The constable's wife, who was a softhearted woman, had picked a bunch of garden flowers, and these had been laid upon the sheet covering the body.

Instructions had been received from England that the body was to be taken home for interment. Deceased's brother would be coming over to travel back with it if all could be made ready. The local undertaker, therefore, entered the mortuary to do what was needed and found the sheet awry and some of the flowers on the floor. The clothes had apparently not been disturbed, and it seemed that nothing was missing. The object of this outrage was not clear unless the miscreant had expected to find Power's wallet there, his smashed wrist watch and the signet ring he habitually wore, but all these things had been locked up in the Gendarmerie safe.

"That's damned odd," said Dr. Farelli when the news reached his ears.

"It's more than odd," said Señor Carboni. "I don't like it."

Later in the morning Monsieur Raoul Rougisson went to the police. He said that he was an ornithologist who was making a quantitative survey of the birds in the Loire Valley; he was staying at the Hotel de la Poste and spent his days wandering about with a pair of binoculars and a notebook or lying up in a hide in woods or fields, watching birds. He was an unremarkable figure of medium height and medium build with very ordinary features; he had thick grey hair and a short bristling beard.

He went into the Gendarmerie at Arnage and asked to see the officer in charge of the enquiry into that fatal car accident. Police Constable Maroche interviewed him.

"There is now," said Maroche, "to be accurate, no officer in charge of that case, for it is closed."

"Then I am come," said Rougisson, "to open it again. Are you the officer in charge?"

Maroche sighed heavily, for if there is one thing more than another calculated to make a policeman sigh, it is having a case reopened when everyone thought it had been comfortably tacked down.

"Why did you not give your testimony yesterday," he asked severely, "when the enquiry was in progress, instead of waiting until now when it is——"

"Because it never occurred to me that those entrusted with the administration of French justice would overlook two plain clues," thundered Rougisson. "I did not expect to have to instruct the Gendarmerie of France and an experienced physician in the performance of their duties! I resent having to do so!"

"Then why do it?"

Rougisson's mouth opened and shut several times, but all he said at last was: "Are you the officer in charge?"

"I am the only officer here," said Maroche mildly, "so presumably I am in charge. What have you to say?"

Rougisson sat down, leaned his elbows on the desk, and said: "Listen. Correct me if I am wrong——"

"Certainly I will."

Rougisson swallowed and began again. "I am told that two witnesses testified that, before the car went off the road, the driver fell suddenly sideways in his seat, letting go of the wheel. Is that so?"

"Both eyewitnesses said he fell sideways; only one said his hands fell from the wheel."

"Thank you. What did this suggest to you or to the Dr. Evette?"

"That the driver had had a seizure, or turned faint, or——"

"Neither," said Rougisson crisply. "Men who faint fall forward or back, not sideways like that. He was shot."

"Shot? Are you mad?"

"Far from it. That is one clue, the falling sideways. The other, which Evette missed, is a bullet in the head."

Maroche came to the natural conclusion that the ornithologist, like so many of these brilliant specialists, was a little peculiar in some ways. He sat back.

"I will inform my superiors of what you say."

"Clever of you," snarled Rougisson. "I have not said it yet."

"Indeed?"

"Listen. You know the small wood on the opposite side of the valley from where the road runs? The Prior's Copse, it is called."

"I have known it for twenty years," said Maroche.

"You know that from it you look across the valley and there, opposite to you, is the hillside and the road? You see it plainly."

"I have done so many times."

"I was there yesterday morning, these binoculars at my eyes, when the red car came down the road from Arnage. Just before—before, Maroche—the car reached that corner, a flock of sparrows flew up suddenly out of the bushes above the road. They went up"—Rougisson gestured—"all ways at once. They were startled. What startled them?"

"The car passing."

"The car, rubbish! Do cars, then, leap off roads to chase birds? Do cars throw stones of themselves—for this driver did not, Maroche. It is not as though he had a small boy with him. No, no, Maroche. Birds do not fear cars passing in the road. There is only one thing that makes a flock of small birds fly up like that——"

"A cat?"

Rougisson almost literally exploded. He banged the desk; he stamped with his feet.

"A gun, fool, a gun, a gun. Fired. When a gun is fired it goes bang. Or crack."

"Or pop," said Maroche interestedly.

"And birds are frightened, so they fly up. Do you understand now?"

"It is an interesting theory and I will put it to my superiors, I promise you, monsieur."

"By the time it has passed through your mental processes it will not be worth hearing."

"That may well be, monsieur."

"What you have got to do—got to do, Maroche—is to insist on that dim-witted old has-been Evette taking another look at that young man's head for a bullet hole. Probably on the right side— yes, on the right. I assume he knows a bullet wound when he sees one?"

"He has served in two wars, monsieur."

"With Napoleon? You will tell him to look for that bullet hole, Maroche, and you will stand over him while he does look, or do you know what I will do?"

"What will you do, monsieur?"

"I will go to the chief newspaper office in Orleans and tell the reporters there that Constable Maroche of Arnage-sur-Loire ignores evidence to save himself trouble."

Maroche blenched.

Rougisson pointed to the telephone upon the desk.

"Ring up Evette," he said, "and tell him to examine the head for a bullet entry wound. Tell him I say 'the head,' because I assume the wound to have been hidden by the hair. Tell him I do him the courtesy to assume that if it had been in the neck or shoulder he would have seen it. Ring up Evette, Maroche, this minute."

Maroche unwillingly obeyed. After all, no harm could be done and it was worth something to quiet this fire-eater. He was, after all, said to be a famous man, and if he talked the reporters would listen.

Dr. Evette at the other end of the telephone heard what Maroche had to say and grunted at intervals.

"Very well," said Evette finally, "I will come and look. If I do not find anything I will send in my little account to the Monsieur Sherlock-'omes Rougisson, pipe and all. I am coming at once, Maroche; meet me at the mortuary."

"Very good, monsieur."

21

Half an hour later Dr. Evette and the constable came out of the mortuary to find Rougisson sitting upon a low wall in the sunshine, waiting for them.

"Well?" said the birdwatcher.

"You were quite right," said the doctor grimly. "I have extracted the bullet."

"I am always right," said Rougisson, and walked away.

"I will ring up Orleans," said Maroche. "The Juge d'Instruction will appoint a time and place for the enquiry."

The doctor fidgeted. "I am not upon the stool of repentance for this," he burst out. "What? A car goes over a cliff and they bring me the body with so many fatal injuries at once that it is a waste of time even to count them all; am I to wear a white sheet because I did not look for a bullet hole as well? Should I hold an autopsy to see if he was poisoned also? Or stabbed with a knife on the end of a pole as he rushed past at sixty kilometres per hour? *Mon Dieu*, that weaselly little birdcatcher——"

"Calm yourself, Monsieur le Docteur, calm yourself," urged Maroche. "The Juge d'Instruction is a sensible man, he does not engage in fantasy. If he thinks the victim was poisoned, there will be an autopsy without any fuss at all. If not, not. I beg Monsieur to calm himself."

"Garr-r-rh!" said Evette, and walked away with rapid strides.

Thomas Elphinstone Hambledon had flown to Paris on the previous evening and had taken an early morning train to Orleans and a country bus from there to Arnage-sur-Loire, arriving at midday. He strolled round the village, looking appreciatively about him, though Heaven knows there is not, as a rule, much in French villages to make the connoisseur of scenic beauty swoon with delight. However, Arnage has the Loire and some pleasant wooded hills, a number of orchards at that time in full blossom, and a really magnificent church. Hambledon walked into the Hotel de la Poste, carrying a suitcase, and asked if they could put him up for a few days. He had been, he said, touring the Loire Valley with friends who had unhappily been recalled to England on account of illness at home, but he himself did not wish to return for another week or so and someone had recommended Arnage as a pleasant quiet place where an overburdened businessman might possess his soul in peace.

"Let Monsieur be content," said the undermanager, whose name was Gallet. "He has come to the right place. One moment while I consult my book——Ah, yes. Of course. A room on the first floor with a window overlooking the river, eh?"

Hambledon approved the room, completed the usual formalities at the reception desk, and then repaired to the bar for a short interval of refreshment before lunch. There were only a few people there, all French except one. There was a young married couple at a table in the window, an older married couple with a sallow little girl on a seat against the wall, an elderly man with a short bristling beard addressing a group at the bar about bird-watching, and one man with his back to Hambledon as he came in. This man was talking to the bartender in French with a strong Spanish accent, and Hambledon recognized immediately the dark head, with the hair going thin on the top, of William Forgan, model-maker. Forgan turned on his stool as Hambledon came in, but neither man made the slightest sign of recognition.

Hambledon asked for a glass of sherry; when the barman served it, he said: "Monsieur is staying in the hotel? Shall I book this to Monsieur?"

"Oh yes, please," said Hambledon. "Room 31." The bartender glanced up sharply and looked down again; no one else took any notice.

"Monsieur is on holiday?" asked Forgan with merely polite interest. Hambledon repeated his story about the interrupted motor tour and added that perhaps the interruption was fortunate for him if not for his anxious friends. "For a man who leads a sedentary life in an office, a motor tour is not really a sufficiently complete change. The fresh air, yes, but where is the exercise? Are there, then, pleasant walks about here?"

"But certainly," said the bartender. "There are many most charming walks."

"I wonder whether there is a map obtainable," said Hambledon.

"Indeed, yes," said the man, producing one from behind the bar and unfolding it. "Monsieur will see the dotted lines are footpaths, of which there are many."

Hambledon leaned over it and Forgan came along the bar to look at it with him.

"I can buy a map like this locally," asked Hambledon, "can I?"

"But certainly, monsieur. At the stationer's, three doors down on this side of the road."

"This path provides a pleasant stroll," said Forgan, indicating one dotted line with a stubby forefinger. "It starts beside the church, passes up the side of a vineyard, and then meanders agreeably through this wood you see indicated. From the top there is obtainable a most admirable view. My patient and I walked up there two days ago; we both enjoyed it immensely." He glanced at his watch, finished his glass of wine, and slid off his high stool. "Excuse me, please. I hope that we shall meet again. Au 'voir, monsieur."

Hambledon watched the square figure cross the lounge and walk up the stairs without a backward glance.

"A very pleasant gentleman," said Hambledon in a low tone to the bartender. "He is staying here also? And what is his name?"

"Monsieur the Dr. Farelli, a Spaniard."

"I thought him Spanish by his speech."

"He is a very famous psychiatrist from Madrid."

"Indeed! And his patient—he spoke of a patient, did he not?"

"Monsieur Carboni, a rich orange grower. They have our best suite," said the bartender. "The poor Monsieur Carboni has been ill, we understand."

"Indeed. I trust he is now quite recovered."

The bartender laughed. "The Dr. Farelli says that he is practically cured. If that is so, I think the poor gentleman must have been very ill. Oranges, we understand."

"Oranges——"

"He has had a nervous breakdown caused by seeing too many oranges. He is still a little——" The man described circles in the air with one finger just abeam of his right ear. "But completely harmless, monsieur."

"Very sad," said Hambledon gravely. He looked a little flushed, but that might have been due to the sherry or even, possibly, to suppressed laughter.

24

CHAPTER 3   *The Birds Flew Up*

Hambledon was strolling across the lounge wondering which was the way to the dining-room, when the hotel door opened and Constable Maroche came in. He looked about him, saw the undermanager, Gallet, sitting in his little office with the door half open, and went across to speak to him. Hambledon had inordinately quick hearing and caught the name of Farelli, so he stayed where he was, lit a cigarette, and picked up a newspaper.

Mumble, mumble, from Gallet.

Maroche said something which included the words "official enquiry by the Juge d'Instruction."

Gallet said quite loudly, "*Mon Dieu!* What for?" and Maroche's answer contained the word "*fusillé.*"

Gallet said, "*Mon Dieu!*" again and there was more muttering. Tommy Hambledon told himself that the cat was out of the bag, and turned over a page. Maroche said quite audibly that the notice to attend must be delivered by himself, personally, and Gallet came with him out of the office to direct him to Dr. Farelli's apartment. Number 19, on the first floor, turn left at the head of the stair.

After lunch, which was excellent—*canard à la solognote*—Hambledon patted his waistcoat approvingly and went out for a walk. He passed the church, strode determinedly up the steep path at the side of the vineyard, and entered the pleasant shade of the woods. Still climbing, the path led him out at last to a gate at the side of a road from which it was quite true that a wide stretch of most agreeable landscape could be seen, but Tommy Hambledon was not at the moment interested in landscape. He leaned his elbows upon the top of the gate, lit a cigarette, and waited.

Presently there approached along the road a tall and dignified automobile; tall because it was of the period when saloon cars were made to accommodate men who not merely owned top hats but habitually wore them, and dignified because it was a Rolls-Royce. It was driven by a chauffeur in uniform, a young man with the thin face, bright enquiring eyes, and cock-sparrow vivacity of a Londoner. Hambledon glanced at him, looked again, and then grinned, for he knew the man.

The Rolls drew up; the chauffeur leapt out, saluting Hambledon as he did so, and opened the car door. Forgan got out first and came forward to meet Hambledon; Campbell followed more slowly because he was encumbered with the sort of long carpetbag with two leather handles such as years ago was used to carry cricket bats, pads, and so on.

"Carry it for you, sir?" said the chauffeur.

"No, no, no. No, I thank you. It likes me to carry it myself."

"Dr. Farelli, I believe," said Hambledon.

Forgan grinned. "Let me introduce my unfortunate patient, Señor Carboni. Señor, this is a distinguished Englishman who desires the honour of your acquaintance."

"I have it here," said the red-haired Campbell, going down on his knees in order to scrabble about in his cricketing bag. It was open upon the ground, and Tommy could see that it was filled with an extraordinary collection of oddments which the afflicted Carboni began to hurl out one after another. A two-pound packet of lump sugar, a large cake of soap, an umbrella wrapped in newspaper, a piece of cheese, a map of the world, and an astronomical chart of the Northern Hemisphere—"very useful in case of being lost at night"—two mousetraps and a fly-flapper, a paper bag containing buns, a copy of *La Vie Parisienne* and another of the *Canary Breeders' Monthly*, three socks and one suspender, several pieces of string, and a box of matches.

"What on earth——" began Tommy Hambledon.

"—are you looking for?" finished Forgan.

"The honour of my acquaintance; I know I put it in here," said Campbell, looking up with such an appalling squint that Hambledon actually recoiled.

"He's very good at it, don't you think?" said Forgan.

"Exceedingly so," said Tommy. "Good afternoon, Arthur, I didn't expect to see you here."

"Life's full of what you don't expect," said the chauffeur, "especially since we was on this lay. Never a dull moment. Reckon I'm training for a tea-leaf carrier if I only knew it."

Since tea leaf rhymes with thief, a tea-leaf carrier is a man who drives a car used by crooks.

"Oh, Arthur, how rude," said Campbell plaintively. "Now you shan't have a lump of sugar."

He hurled the things back into the bag, gave it to the chauffeur to put in the car, and straightened up.

"Let's go for a stroll in the wood, shall we?" he said. "We are a little conspicuous here, and Forgan and I have some odds and ends to tell you. What about the car?"

"I should fill her up," said Arthur. "She's a good old bus, sir," to Hambledon, "but what she takes in juice 'ud float Noah's Ark."

"Do that," said Forgan, "and come back here in an hour's time. Don't get the petrol in Arnage; go on towards Orleans somewhere. Have you got enough money?"

"Is there such a thing?" asked the chauffeur, but he did not seem to need any, for he sprang into the car and drove away while the three men turned into the wood.

"Where on earth did you get that chariot?" asked Hambledon.

"Picked it up cheap in Bordeaux," said Forgan. "Since we were supposed to have come here from Spain, we thought it simpler if we just came here from Spain, if you get me. Passport stamps all correct and so forth."

"Would you mind beginning at the beginning," said Hambledon, "because I have no idea what's been happening, where, or why, since you left. Power only reported about another job he was on."

"We went to Paris and met Power first of all," said Campbell. "He said that he thought the centre of this conspiracy was either at or near Arnage. He also said that he thought there were other centres elsewhere, but this was the only one he'd located. So would we settle in Arnage. Well, if Forgan and I can't be English, the only thing we can convincingly be is Spaniards, as you know. So we went from Paris to Barcelona, across to St.

27

Sebastian, and back into France at Irún. We had a night in Bordeaux, and there we saw this, which you rightly call a chariot, more or less running round wagging its tail looking for a kind master, so we bought it."

"We were told it had belonged to an English milord," said Forgan, "and we believed that at once. It has that air."

"It's too old for anyone who can afford to buy petrol," said Campbell, "and too heavy on petrol for anyone who can't. Having got the car, we reorganized ourselves to fit it and wired for Arthur to come out. We've shut the shop so he'd nothing to do, anyway, but you should have seen his face when he found he had to wear uniform. His idea of suitable dress in which to drive a Rolls is a sinister felt hat and a phosphorescent tie."

"We had to tell him that it wasn't uniform at all," said Forgan, "it was really a disguise, because we were tracking down the infamous Black Cobra gang of international criminals, and he swallowed that hook, line, and sinker. Now, dammit, it seems we weren't far out, can you beat it?"

"Very awkward," said Hambledon, "but is that really the case?"

"Power said so. Before we go any further, there's a little more to tell you about Power." Campbell told the full story of Power's apparent accident and gave Hambledon the cartridge case they had found on the site. "Before we left poor Power, we went through his pockets hoping for something enlightening, but we weren't very lucky. There was this little notebook."

It was a very small note pad about three inches by two, in which thin sheets of squared paper were held together by a spiral wire at the top. Page one held only a scribbled telephone number with no indication as to whose it was. The other pages were virgin, but slipped between them was a small square cut from a glossy picture postcard, and on the square was a very nice fingerprint.

"The telephone number is not very informative to us," said Forgan, "though no doubt one could find out. Ring up and say, 'Is that the Megatherium Stores? Ladies' underwear, please.' But we thought we'd leave that to you."

"We were a little afraid we might get it," said Campbell. "Ladies' underwear, I mean."

"So we left it to you," repeated Forgan.

"We are shy men," added Campbell.

"I expect I can find out without involving myself in embarrassment," said Hambledon. "I shall have to get in touch with the police, not the local John Hop but the head office in Orleans. They can find out for me."

"There was this, too," said Campbell. "Tucked away in an inside pocket."

He handed Hambledon a small oval silver box about an inch and a half long by an inch wide and quite shallow, with a formal engraved pattern on the lid; such small silver boxes are commonly to be seen in the windows of those who sell secondhand jewellery.

"Snuff, or patches?" asked Tommy, and opened it.

Inside were three dried beans, cream-coloured with irregular markings of dark brown; grocers call them Madagascar beans. There was nothing else in the box; Hambledon tipped them out in his hand and turned them about.

"Any comments?" he asked.

"No comments," said Forgan.

"No comments," echoed Campbell.

Hambledon put them back in the box and shut the lid. "Now then. What, if anything, did Power tell you about this job? And do you know anything about this fingerprint?"

The model-makers looked at each other and then at Tommy Hambledon.

"First question first," said Forgan. "Do you know anything about the Stock Exchange?"

"Only a lot of funny stories."

"Or about stocks and shares generally?"

"No. Precious little. Why?"

"Nor did we," said Campbell, "until Power instructed us. If you can make shares go down by starting rumours about the stability of the company, you can buy them cheap. Then, when it turns out the company's all right after all, the shares rise in value, you sell yours and make money. Simple."

"Quite," said Hambledon. "Are you trying to tell me that Power's earth-shaking conspiracy was just a group of men manipulating shares——"

"Oh no. That was just a simple example to show the way the thing was worked. Like illustrating the changes in the seasons with an orange on a skewer to represent the earth and an electric torch for the sun. Nor have these people operated in England so far as he knew, at least not yet. Pass, Stock Exchange, all's well. They operated abroad where rules are less hampering and more easily evaded and where panics are more easily started. Think of a country where there are oil wells, a greedy but unsophisticated ruling class, and an excitable but illiterate peasantry. All the perfumes of Arabia, in short. Well now, if you start riots, murder a few people, and chase out engineers and technicians, what happens to the shares of that oil company?"

"Even I," said Tommy, "know the answer to that one."

"But the oil's still there, all the same," concluded Campbell. "As a matter of fact, Abadan was a bit overdone as you may remember, but I expect even Abadan will rise from its depths one of these days. Well, that's the sort of scale on which these people work, according to Power. Now then. Let us move on from the affairs of mere companies to the various governmental bonds and stocks. We all saw what happened on the New York Stock Exchange when the news came out that President Eisenhower had had a heart attack."

Hambledon's face showed a mixture of emotions, mainly incredulity and disgust, but at this last suggestion incredulity took control.

"Are you seriously suggesting——"

"Great heavens, no," said Forgan a little irritably. "That was a natural illness, of course. Power was only pointing out the effect it had."

"He went on to say," added Campbell, "that the same result would be attained by a well-selected murder."

"Besides," continued Forgan, "the surprising effect on international relations if the blame for the murder could be firmly nailed to a sensitive spot. Just when we're all getting so nice and matey, too."

"Dear me," said Hambledon thoughtfully.

"Just what we said. Now, about the fingerprint. On the morning when he was killed," said Campbell, "we were all sitting in the lounge after breakfast. Power strolled across and said that he was going to cash a traveller's cheque at the office and thereafter proposed to loiter in the hotel garden. If we would join him there he would tell us a bit more. He then strolled across to the bureau and was waiting for the clerk to attend to him when his attention was attracted by a stand of glossy picture postcards. He took one out and, when the clerk came to him, he bought it. He slipped it between the pages of a paper he was carrying and galloped upstairs, not waiting to cash his cheque."

"Campbell and I were playing cat's cradle with a piece of string, and at this point he showed signs of getting annoyed with it."

"The problem would not come out," said Campbell gloomily.

"So I said, 'Let us go and walk in the garden——' "

" '—and look for worms.' I like worms. Do you?"

"For pity's sake," said Hambledon.

"A few minutes later Power came out in a state of reasonably well-concealed excitement. He said he'd recognized a fingerprint," said Forgan. "Can one believe that?"

"In Power's case, yes," said Hambledon. "I'll tell you in a minute. Please go on."

"Recognized a print on the postcard, so he bought it and went up to his room to compare it with a photostat he'd got. He said it was the same and that he couldn't wait to talk to us then because he was going to rush it in to the police at Orleans to get them to send it to Paris for checking, perhaps by now they knew whose it was."

"This being more than we could bear," said Campbell languidly, "I detained him in the act of departure and besought him to come clean. He said hurriedly that some time ago there was a murder in Paris of a man who was a well-known financier. Power was in with the Sûreté on this. The body was removed to the mortuary, the flat sealed up, and a policeman left on guard outside. In spite of that, the flat was ransacked in the night; when the detectives went in, in the morning, the place was a strew from end to end. The only clue to the unknown visitor was one fingerprint, and even that was not in police records. 'Now,' said Power, 'it's turned up in Arnage. Good-bye, I'm off.' He then left us abruptly."

"He went towards the lock-ups," said Forgan. "So, as it was

plainly no use our hanging about that excessively uninspired garden, we went for a walk. We were surprised when, a whole hour later, we saw him driving hell-for-leather on the road to Orleans."

"What had delayed him?" asked Hambledon.

"Car trouble of some kind, presumably," said Campbell. "I don't know."

"I think I shall try to find out," said Tommy. "It might possibly have been something arranged to give the murderer time to get under cover in the bushes."

"I wish you luck," said Forgan, "if it was something done to the MG itself. It's a heap of twisted metal caked with ashes."

Hambledon shrugged his shoulders and changed the subject. "You asked if a fingerprint could be recognized on sight; the answer is yes, if you've made a study of them and have a photographic sort of memory. Superintendent Cherrill, when he was at Scotland Yard, was said to know hundreds of them. He'd recognize them as you or I would recognize faces. I'm not suggesting that Power was anywhere near Cherrill's class, because he stands alone, but Power had made a hobby of it from boyhood and had studied up types and characteristics. Besides, you must remember that he's seen the print in Paris under mysterious and exciting circumstances; he would naturally have memorized it and would almost certainly recognize it if he saw it again. Yes, that's credible enough. I wonder——"

"What?"

"Who the murdered financier was and what he was playing at."

"Would that affair," said Forgan, "be what started Power on the track of all this?"

"I don't know," said Hambledon. "It did start in Paris, or so I gathered. I'll go and talk to the police. I might even go to Paris and have a word with an old friend of mine, Letord of the Sûreté."

"The enquiry is being held here tomorrow morning," said Forgan. "I've just had a command to attend."

"Yes, I'll wait till that's over."

Early the following day the Juge d'Instruction came out from Orleans to hold an enquiry into the death by violence of Alan

Power, a British subject. A Juge d'Instruction is not very like an English coroner, although he takes the stage upon similar occasions; he is more like the Scottish Procurator Fiscal, since both are a part of the police organization. An English coroner is a part of the English judiciary, which is entirely separate from the police and long may they remain so.

To return to the Juge d'Instruction. He arrives upon the scene as soon after the tragedy as is conveniently possible; he causes to be gathered together everybody who was at or near the scene at the time and, then and there and in the presence of each other, he takes evidence on oath, asks questions, cross-examines, and generally puts through the mincing machine every single person present, whether they know anything about the affair or not. He proceeds upon the assumption that everyone is guilty unless he can prove himself innocent, since this is a maxim of French justice. In a word, an enquiry by a Juge d'Instruction into a case of murder is no joke.

The enquiry opened at half-past nine in the morning. Hambledon was not there, since the public are not admitted, nor was the neurotic Señor Carboni. Witnesses called were Pierre Lacroix, manager of the Hotel de la Poste; the Spanish doctor, Benito Farelli; the lorry driver; Police Constable Jean Maroche; Dr. Alexandre Evette of Arnage-sur-Loire; and Monsieur Raoul Rougisson of Paris, an ornithologist.

Lacroix was the first witness. He was a small man with a comfortably rounded figure, a round pink face, very smooth golden hair, and gold-rimmed spectacles. He had a timid and self-effacing manner and was plainly terrified of the Juge d'Instruction, a large man with menacing eyebrows. Lacroix testified that the deceased was a Monsieur Alan Power, an Englishman, who had stayed at his hotel the night before the tragedy. Yes, he had stayed at the Hotel de la Poste on several occasions before but never for long at a time; a night, two nights, that was all. Monsieur Power had said that he worked in Paris and came to Arnage for an occasional breath of fresh air. No, he seemed to have no enemies, why should he? He was a pleasant and friendly young man, and Lacroix was prostrated with horror when he heard of the tragic occurrence. Everyone in the hotel was grieved.

"He habitually drove himself about in the red sports car?"

"But certainly, Monsieur le Juge. He was said to be a very good driver, although he habitually drove fast."

"The car was well known locally? It would be readily recognized as being Monsieur Power's?"

Lacroix looked surprised. "It was the only car like that to be seen in the district—an English car and of that conspicuous colour."

The Juge d'Instruction nodded. "Have you anything else to say touching upon this matter?"

"Only that—if it has any bearing—that it may have been my fault, or rather my misfortune, that he was driving so fast that morning. I was about setting forth to go to Orleans in my car for marketing, when I had a puncture exactly outside the lock-up where the red car was kept. My spare was already punctured. I therefore sent for the *garagiste* here to repair the punctures and he accordingly came up. He jacked up the car, removed the wheels, and took them down to his workshop for repair, leaving the car upon the jack. I understand that the man was but just out of sight when Monsieur Power rushed out of the hotel saying that he wanted his car at once, but at once, to go to Orleans on business. He was, I am told quite angry about it, but my staff could do nothing, my car being upon the jack, as Monsieur le Juge will understand. I was not there myself, I had gone out upon an errand. When the *garagiste* brought back my wheels, Monsieur Power was approaching the end of his patience. I hear that as soon as the way was clear he leapt into his car and drove away even faster than usual. So it may be, Monsieur le Juge, that that was the reason why he was driving even faster than usual and failed to take that corner."

The Juge d'Instruction looked under his drawn brows at the twittering Lacroix.

"And why are you telling me all this, Lacroix?"

"I felt—I could not but feel—I could not reconcile it with my conscience not to avow——"

"You may lay your conscience to rest, Lacroix. The deceased's speed had nothing to do with his death. If he had stopped still on that corner he would have died all the same."

"What—I do not understand——"

"Next witness."

Farelli and the lorry driver gave the same evidence as before. They were questioned closely about details and finally asked if they had seen anyone else about or heard anything like a shot fired. Farelli said he had not and the lorry driver said that anyone driving that vehicle of his would not hear also a battery of cannon. Police Constable Maroche's evidence was purely formal.

Dr. Alexandre Evette was roughly handled for not having found the bullet wound earlier, but defended himself with spirit. He and the Juge d'Instruction had known each other for many years, and honours were considered to be even.

Finally, Monsieur Raoul Rougisson, who repeated the story he had told the constable, and the Juge d'Instruction scowled at him.

"What excuse have you to offer, Rougisson, for not having given this evidence before?"

"Why should I? These eyewitnesses saw all that I did and more, for all I saw was a flock of small birds fly up. They saw the poor young man fall sideways, they saw his hands slip from the driving wheel. If they did not see the birds also, I cannot tell why not. It was not until I heard that the death was said to be an accident that I realized my testimony was required."

"Every eyewitness, Rougisson, is required by law to give his or her evidence in such a case as this. It is not left to the witness's own discretion whether to testify or not."

"I will remember what Monsieur le Juge has said, the next time I am involved in a murder case."

"If you are impertinent, Rougisson, you will be made to regret it. Leave the witness stand and sit down over there. I wish to ask another question of the witness Farelli. Dr. Ferelli, you were in a position to see these birds fly up. Did you, in fact, do so?"

Forgan thought for a moment and shook his head. "They might have done so and I not notice it," he said. "It would mean nothing to me. I am a townsman. The last witness is an ornithologist and studies the habits of birds."

The Juge d'Instruction announced his decision. "This is a case of murder. There is insufficient evidence at the moment to show who committed the crime. The police have the affair in hand. Thank you, gentlemen."

The witnesses filed out, leaving the Juge d'Instruction with his entourage of police. Among these was the Superintendent of Police in Orleans, who was staring out of the window and muttering to himself. The Juge d'Instruction crossed over to him and laid a hand upon his shoulder.

"What is that you are mumbling there?"

"I said," answered the Superintendent, " 'Not another Dominici case. Kind heaven, not another Dominici case.' "

"Heaven avert it," said the Juge d'Instruction fervently.

There had been, at the enquiry, a thin and sallow young man with a breast pocket glittering with the clips of ball-point pens. He was a junior reporter for an Orleans paper who had trailed wearily out to Arnage at the call of duty, expecting nothing but a dull road-accident enquiry which would get four lines in his paper. The path of duty looked like turning into the way of glory, for he had got a scoop. He slipped out of the room the moment the enquiry finished, dashed to a telephone, and rang up his office. Mysterious Tragedy at Arnage-sur-Loire. English Motorist Shot Dead.

"Get the story," said the sub-editor. "Visit the scene. Interview everybody. Photograph the small birds and the wrecked car. Do your stuff properly, or I'll——"

The young man bolted out of the telephone box and began to run, and then a thought struck him. He looked up a number in his notebook, returned to the telephone box, and asked for a London number. He had some time to wait for it, but he did not seem to mind, and at last he was connected.

"That Exchange Telegraph and Central News? Peyret, of the *Orleans Intelligencer*, speaking from Arnage-sur-Loire. An Englishman has been shot dead in his car; it is murder, it is not known who did it——"

CHAPTER 4 *Seeker after Truth*

THE WITNESSES drifted out into the village street, and Lacroix instantly hurried away. The others stood about, talking, and certain of the local inhabitants drew near to ask what was the result. Hambledon came down the street and exhibited horror and shock in appropriate proportions on hearing the news.

"But how did it all come out?" he asked. Forgan and Dr. Evette told him in a sort of duet while Rougisson stood off a little and registered superiority. Hambledon addressed him.

"Excuse me, monsieur. We are staying in the same hotel, I think. I hear that it was your evidence which turned a sad but common road accident into a murder."

"Someone," said Rougisson, "had to direct these simpletons upon the right path." His eyes fell as though by accident upon Drs. Evette and Farelli.

"Monsieur must be unusually observant," said Hambledon admiringly.

"Monsieur, the practice of birdwatching induces the habit of observation. I wish you good day."

He nodded casually and walked away while Hambledon rejoined the others. Evette was spluttering.

"That—that—that——" he said, and added what, in his opinion, Rougisson was.

"I am inclined to agree with you," said Dr. Farelli primly. "An almost psychopathic tendency to over-self-appreciation."

Since the sight of Forgan being prim always induced in Hambledon an almost psychopathic tendency to laugh, he excused himself.

"I am going along to buy some cigarettes," he said. "We shall perhaps meet for a moment at the bar before lunch, Dr. Farelli? Dr. Evette, we shall meet again soon, I hope."

"It will be a pleasure," said Evette, "which is more than I should say about some people. Garr-r-rh!" He got into his car and drove away.

Hambledon went into a small shop outside which was displayed the large red cigar rampant, the sign which, in France, means: "Tobacco sold here." The moment he was inside it was obvious that the excellent woman who kept the shop had heard the news, for she was dabbing her eyes, patting her bosom, and exhibiting agitation.

"Monsieur must excuse. I have heard some shocking news, I am upset. Cigarettes? *He* came in here to buy cigarettes, the poor young man. So pleasant, such charm, he reminded me of my son."

"You knew Monsieur Power, madame?"

"But yes, as one knows a pleasant customer who calls in occasionally. He drove that little red car—oh, to terrify—but now they say he is murdered."

"So I also have heard."

"When I heard that he was killed driving too fast, I was sorry but, you understand, not surprised. He passed here the morning he was killed, going *comme au diable*, as we say. I was serving Monsieur Rougisson with his tobacco and we remarked together upon his pace. It was terrible, like a flash he passed, and ten minutes later—alas!"

"Monsieur Rougisson?"

"Monsieur does not know him? The bird man. He is staying at the Hotel de la Poste."

"I know the man you mean," said Hambledon. "I am staying there too. May I have fifty, madame? And how much?"

Hambledon walked back to the hotel and encountered Forgan and Campbell in the garden.

"Something funny about that fellow Rougisson," he said, and repeated what he had just been told.

"If he didn't see the birds fly up," said Forgan slowly, "how did he know that Power was shot?"

"Ask me another," said Tommy. "He couldn't possibly have done it himself, that's an impeccable alibi."

"He'll bear watching," said Forgan.

As for the afflicted Señor Carboni, he sang in a pleasing light baritone that charming if morbid aria from *Trovatore:* "Ah! *che la morte . . .*" He accompanied it with a few dance steps and some graceful ballet gestures, and his attendant removed him from public view. It was, in any case, lunch time.

The police, of course, had the .22 bullet which Dr. Evette had extracted from the head of the deceased, and Maroche started at once upon a round of the village and immediate neighbourhood to collect .22 rifles and pistols. A ballistics expert would then find out which, if any, of those weapons fired that bullet. Maroche returned home tired out more with argument than exercise, for the French peasant does not readily co-operate with the police. His bag was four rifles and one pistol.

Hambledon went to bed that night with his Luger automatic under his pillow as usual; his more intimate friends who knew his habits used to say that if for any reason the gun was not under the pillow Hambledon always dreamed that he was walking across the forecourt of Buckingham Palace, stark naked, at the time of the Changing of the Guard. A sense of nudity.

He lay awake for some time brooding over the inquest but finally put out the light and went to sleep. He woke again some time later, though it was still quite dark; as he wondered what had awakened him he heard the church clock strike two and was suddenly quite certain that there was someone in the room. He sat up and slipped his hand under his pillow.

"No use, monsieur," said a quiet voice, speaking French. "I have your gun. I was a little afraid you might be impulsive."

Hambledon turned the bedside switch of the electric light, but that also availed him nothing.

"I have removed the bulb," went on the quiet voice, dropping to a whisper. "Still, as we shall want some light, let us try this."

A brilliant beam of light from a powerful electric torch shone straight into Hambledon's eyes and blinded him completely. He could shut his eyes as some relief from the glare or shade them with his hands, but he could see nothing but a yard or so of his own bed and the bed head behind him.

"Look," whispered the voice. A hand came into the beam of light, and it was holding a Luger automatic; probably, Hambledon thought, his own. He was quite right, it was. "I merely wished to convince you that I was not bluffing."

The hand disappeared and the light wavered about a little, as though the man holding it were looking for something.

"Ah," said the voice in a relieved whisper, "the very thing. One of your shoes. Now, if I put that on this table here"—a bumping noise—"and arrange the torch in it, so, I shall have a hand free to do what I came to do."

"Who the devil are you?"

"You might, with complete accuracy, describe me as a seeker after truth," said the whispering voice.

"Indeed. Not after loose change and small items of personal jewellery?"

"There is no need to be rude, monsieur. I am not, in point of fact, particularly interested either in you or in your portable property. I am more interested in your predecessor."

"My predecessor? Where?"

"In this room. Its last occupant was the unfortunate young Englishman who was killed in that car crash two days ago."

"Indeed?" said Hambledon. "I did not know that. In any case, I believe his things to have been packed up and handed over to the police."

There was no answer to this, only a scratchy noise upon the wall, followed by the sound of tearing paper. Hambledon had searched rooms often enough himself to know exactly what the man was doing; he was taking the two pictures down from the wall and tearing off the paper backing to see whether anything had been hidden inside. It was irritating to think that this man, who was, to Hambledon, entirely concealed in a pit of darkness behind that painful glare, could himself see very comfortably indeed by reflected light.

"It is not, then, so large," said Tommy conversationally, "this object for which you seek."

"Please keep your voice down."

"Why? I might be talking to myself, you know, or even in my sleep. People do, I believe," said Hambledon in his normal voice. If this man were tiresome enough to come and hiss at him in the middle of the night, he certainly was not going to hiss back as though they were a couple of loving cobras. Curse the fellow.

"Could you please hurry up and have done? I shall have spots before the eyes for days to come."

There was an electric fire in the fender before the empty fireplace, and it scraped on the tiles as the man moved it. "I think I have seen Monsieur in Paris."

"It is possible. I occasionally visit Paris."

"Monsieur was being conducted by detectives into the offices of the Sûreté, if it is not tactless to mention it."

Hambledon's mind went back to various occasions upon which he had indeed visited the Sûreté in the company of detectives, though not, as this whisperer appeared to think, as a captive.

"Even the French police," said Tommy blandly, "make mistakes sometimes, do they not?"

There came a tapping at the door and a voice outside. "Monsieur! Is all well with Monsieur? Monsieur, please!"

"Do not answer," whispered the man urgently, but there came the rattle of a passkey in the lock and he turned towards the window. The door opened, admitting a certain amount of subdued light from the landing outside and also the night porter, a large man. He tried the switch by the door, but as that merely actuated the same lamp as the bedside light, there was no result.

"Come in," said Hambledon, but there was no need, for the porter came in with a rush as though he had been pushed from behind and put his foot on something that first rolled and then went off pop like an inflated paper bag. Of course, the light bulb. The porter staggered, clutched at the table, and knocked down the electric torch, which went out. It was possible to see dimly the figure of a man in the act of climbing out of the window; the porter leapt at him and seized him by the wrist, which had the effect of making him drop Hambledon's gun with a clatter upon the floorboards.

"Let go," said the man outside the window. He descended several steps of what must plainly be a ladder outside and tried to twist his hand out of the porter's grip. Hambledon scrambled out of bed and rushed to the window, but it was almost entirely blocked by the porter's massive shoulders and he could do nothing.

"Come *up*," said the porter, grunting, and heaved, but the intruder resisted violently, and in the same moment there was a sliding crash outside as the ladder fell down. The man's whole weight swung upon his arm, the porter's hand slipped, and his captive dropped to the ground twelve feet below. There followed immediately the crack of a gun and the sound of running feet.

"Now who's shot what?" asked the porter in an exasperated voice. He leaned out of the window; Hambledon, groping on the floor for his Luger, got his fingers trodden on and complained loudly.

"Looks like someone lying down there," said the porter, taking no notice. "Can't see who——"

"Get off my hand, you oaf!"

"Oh! I regret. Have I hurt Monsieur?" The porter withdrew from the window and looked round. "Where is Monsieur Lacroix?"

"Lacroix?" said Hambledon, rubbing his fingers. "Haven't seen him."

"He came up with me," said the Porter. "He was urging me on."

Hambledon thought that urging somebody else on was precisely what one would expect of Lacroix, but did not say so.

"There's a light over the washbasin," he said. "Switch it on, please." When this had been done Hambledon pulled on his dressing gown, thrust his feet into his slippers, picked up his Luger, and led the way downstairs at a canter, with the porter at his heels. As they passed through the lounge on their way to the door Hambledon noticed in passing the neatly rounded form of Lacroix at the bar. He was drinking hurriedly from a glass; in the other hand was a bottle of cognac, *grand fine*.

"Poor little man," said Hambledon to himself, "all upset. He would be."

The night porter snatched up a torch, and together he and Hambledon went out into the night, not so dark as it had been, since lights were going up in most of the windows and from many of them heads leaned out, passionately asking questions.

Along the front of the hotel, round to the right——

"There," said the porter, and trained the light on a huddled form face-downwards on the ground. When they turned it over he uttered a loud exclamation.

"It is Monsieur Rougisson! The bird man! A guest in this hotel. What a misfortune, what a disaster! The miscreant, in escaping, has shot him!"

"What was he doing out here," asked Hambledon, "at this time of night?"

"He went out soon after midnight, monsieur, after birds, as he told me, the poor man."

"Birds? In the dark? What sort of birds?"

"Owls, monsieur, naturally."

"Oh, naturally," said Hambledon.

There came upon the scene a number of dancing lights, these being electric torches in the hands of various excited people in all stages of informal dress from pyjamas onwards. The first person actually to reach the scene of the tragedy was, however, the undermanager, Gallet. He joined the porter in a duet recitative of "What a misfortune," etc., and the audience gathered round, asking questions. The answers, summarized, were (a) yes, he is dead, (b) he has been shot, (c) Monsieur Rougisson, the well-known ornithologist, (d) an intruder who entered the hotel by means of an open window, (e) we have not the slightest idea at present but no doubt the police—— At this moment the police arrived in the substantial form of Constable Maroche. He took one long look at the dead man, turned to Gallet, and said: "Summon for me, if you please, the doctor by telephone. Thereafter, kindly inform Detective Inspector Vidal in Room 51 in this hotel."

"Certainly," said Gallet, and turned to go indoors; Hambledon went with him.

"Murder in Arnage-sur-Loire," said Gallet in a dark voice, "is bad enough, but murder in the Hotel de la Poste also, it is too much."

"Two too much," agreed Hambledon.

"What it will give me to do," lamented Gallet, "as though my days were already filled with dreamy inertia."

"Surely," said Hambledon, "your manager, Monsieur Lacroix——"

"Manager," said Gallet, stopping suddenly and seizing Tommy by the arm in order to hiss into his ear, "manager, indeed! A figurehead, a dummy, a—a—— Listen, monsieur. All our manager concerns himself with is the marketing and the cooking."

"Then I congratulate him," said Tommy firmly.

"But all that is for the chef! For the chef, I say! Does this

Monsieur Lacroix deal with the correspondence? Receive guests? Supervise the servants? Organize the organization? Deal with the emergencies? Ha, ha," said the undermanager with a hollow sardonic laugh.

"But who appointed him, then, or is he——"

"Messieurs the proprietors! Me, I have been here in this hotel seven year and these managers, they come and go, but am I appointed in their stead? No, of course not. I am not the nephew of the wife of the proprietors, or the husband of the cousin, or the brother-in-law of the aunt. I spit." He did so. "Now, when an emergency occurs, you see? 'Gallet, forward! I am upset, I do not feel well. I have the fluctuations at the stomach.' Bah!"

"Too bad," said Hambledon, "but, about the doctor and the police——"

"Monsieur is right," said Gallet gloomily. "I run," and he did so, leaving Tommy to rub his ear, for the effect of "Bah!" delivered at a range of half an inch should be felt to be believed. He then stubbed his toe painfully against the corner of a rockery, remembered that he was wearing only bedroom slippers, and followed Gallet into the hotel. Sounds of energetic telephoning floated out from the office; Hambledon passed it by and went to the bar, where the despised Lacroix was sitting on a high stool with a glass in his hand, staring into vacancy. Hambledon addressed him.

"Good evening, Monsieur Lacroix."

The man leapt nervously and turned to face him.

"G-good evening."

"I think," said Hambledon, "that I should like a cognac too, please."

"The bartender is not on duty," said Lacroix. "I will get it for you myself." He made a long arm for a glass, filled it with a shaking hand, and pushed it along the bar.

"Thank you. I believe I have to thank you also for bringing the night porter up to my room to deal with that intruder. I did not see you then to thank you, but the porter told me you came up with him."

"I did not enter the room," said Lacroix in a weak voice. "I am not a man of violence; besides, what does one pay night porters for?"

44

"Exactly. Tell me, how did you know the man was there?"

"I was taking a turn in the garden before retiring. I saw the ladder. I returned at once."

"I'll bet you did," said Tommy to himself, and sipped his cognac.

"Monsieur," said Lacroix after a moment, "what did the man want? Your watch, and so on, I suppose?"

"No, he did not touch them. He was searching the room for something."

Lacroix actually looked interested. "The room? Why and what for?"

"What for, I do not know. Why, because the Englishman Power had previously occupied it, so the intruder himself said."

"Indeed. Did you see him?"

Hambledon explained why he had not. Gallet, having finished his telephoning, came out of the office, threw a contemptuous glance towards the bar, and hurried out into the garden. Lacroix emptied his glass and rose unsteadily to his feet.

"I shall go to my room, if Monsieur will excuse me. I am upset. I am not well."

"But if the police wish to interview you——"

"They can do so in the morning." Lacroix turned away from the bar, hesitated, turned back, and took the cognac bottle from the bar. Without another word, and holding the bottle firmly to his chest, he wandered vaguely across the lounge, through the service door, and out of sight. The door swung to behind him.

"Well, well," said Hambledon.

He made his way towards the stairs, only to be intercepted by a vivid brunette in orange trousers, for the lounge was beginning to fill with excited people.

"Monsieur! Forgive, please, my importunity, but what in point of fact has happened?"

"A man has been shot, mademoiselle."

"*Formidable!* An accident?"

"I did not see it happen, mademoiselle."

"Who was he, does anyone know?"

"The ornithologist, Monsieur Rougisson."

"What? The little man with the beard? He was staying here, yes? *Formidable.* For me, I do not wonder."

"Indeed, mademoiselle? May I ask why?"

"I know," she said, rolling enormous dark eyes at Hambledon. "He was giving his so-famous talk upon the Lesser Shrike and his victim could not get away. So he shot him. Me, I nearly shot him myself yesterday but that I had no gun. Otherwise I would have wallowed him in his gore without a mo-oment's compunction!"

"*Formidable*," said Hambledon, and was edging away when Forgan came in at the garden door, towing behind him his patient, who had an armful of orange lilies.

"Farelli," he was saying, "Farelli, please do not hurry me so. I cannot hurry before breakfast. Besides, I must speak to the waiter; there was not enough glue in my coffee this morning— yesterday morning. Ah!" He wrenched himself free and fell on his knees in front of the brunette in the trousers. "Look, I have been out in the dawn to pick lilies for you to match your—your draperies. Simone, may I call you Simone?"

"It is not my name, but let not that impede Monsieur," said the girl, giggling.

"Indeed, indeed I will not." Carboni arranged the lilies round the brunette's feet and stood back to admire the result. Farelli took him firmly by the arm. "Simone——"

"Thank you a thousand times," she said, and stooped to pick them up. "I adore orange, don't——"

"Orange!" cried the invalid. "Orange? Oh-h-h——" He broke into a wild sort of stamping dance, and the crowd parted to give him room. Farelli, as it were, dancing with him, guided him towards the stairs, and together they stamped and capered up them. Farelli paused at the top.

"But perfectly harmless," he said earnestly.

"*Formidable*," said the lady. Hambledon turned away and found his elbow taken by an Englishman who was staying in the hotel.

"Oddly reminiscent," he said, "of the Highland Fling, that dance. Don't you agree?"

"I do," said Hambledon, and meant it.

HAMBLEDON RETURNED to his bedroom and looked longingly at his bed, but there was no knowing when the French police would wish to start asking him the endless questions they certainly would ask, and it would be intolerable to be hauled out of sleep twice in one night. He sighed deeply and began to dress; he was only half done when there came a knock at his door.

"Who is there?"

"Le Docteur Farelli."

"Come in!"

Forgan entered and shut the door behind him.

"Officially," he said in a low voice, "I've come to borrow some aspirins. Unofficially, could you come to our suite? Campbell's got a story to tell you. We thought it better if you came to us, if you don't mind. For one thing, we've got a private sitting-room, and for another, Campbell's rather a conspicuous figure to be paying calls in the middle of a night when everyone's wandering about the corridors."

"Certainly. Just a moment while I finish dressing. What's happening downstairs? Police starting enquiries?"

"Not yet, I think," said Forgan, returning to the door. "Do you know where we are? To the left here, round the corner and down the long corridor. We're the last door on the left. *Mille remerciements, monsieur*," he added for the benefit of any who might be within earshot when the door opened.

"It is nothing," said Hambledon correctly.

Forgan went away, and five minutes later Tommy followed him.

"We thought it might come in useful at some time," said

Campbell, "as well as enhancing my peculiar reputation, if I wandered about at night sometimes. The night porter very kindly and tactfully escorted me back to my room two nights ago, so I kissed him on both cheeks and gave him a thousand francs. Next time I'll give him two thousand francs and no kisses, it'll be cheaper. I go out by a window."

"One of these?"

"No. One we spotted from the garden. Round the end of the hotel here there's a sort of lean-to roof attached to the wall and a small window over it, the window of the housemaid's cupboard. Under the lean-to there are sheltered the truck which takes the luggage to the station, a wheelbarrow, a lawn mower, and such oddments, and along the wall there hangs a ladder on a couple of hooks. The scene is set. The window opens noiselessly; it has been oiled. A head peers cautiously out, the auburn head of a handsome Highlander. He pauses, for he hears a noise. I have your enthralled interest?"

"Go on," said Hambledon, "I can scarcely breathe."

"Good. The noise came from under the lean-to, so I waited. It was not loud, the noise, scratching and muffled bumps. Then a dimly seen figure emerged carrying the ladder. Who the man was I haven't the faintest idea. He backed away, settled the ladder a bit more comfortably, and padded off, so I climbed out of the window, slid down the roof, stepped on to the porter's truck, and, only pausing to put on my shoes, I went in pursuit. I say, that was a long sentence."

"He went round the house, I suppose," said Tommy, "and planted his ladder against my window."

"That's right. I knew which was yours because you've got Power's room. I wondered whether I ought to rush back through the house and warn you, and while my mind was slowly revolving the man climbed up the ladder and got in. Well, I thought you could look after yourself and, in any case, the nearest way to your room was up his ladder and take him in the rear, so I retired into a bush and waited. A dim light appeared in your window."

"Dim? Oh, that would be while he was taking my gun away and unscrewing the bulb out of the bedside lamp. When I woke up he turned the torch straight in my face and I couldn't see a thing. Tell me, how much could you see outside? It was pretty dark, wasn't it?"

"Yes, but one's eyes got used to it and the outside walls here are white. I could see silhouettes against it, and the ladder standing up. Then the light in your room got much brighter."

"That's when he turned it on me."

"No doubt. Some time passed and nothing happened until a certain uproar broke out in your room. Oh, and the light went out. The fellow's legs came a few steps down the ladder, but the rest of him appeared to be detained by something——"

"The night porter."

"Oh, and there was a clatter of something falling on boards."

"My Luger. He dropped it."

"Yes. There was a certain amount of chattery of the 'Let go!' 'Come here!' type and some struggling, and then a dark figure appeared round the corner of the house and rushed along the path towards the ladder."

"Are you quite sure," said Hambledon, "that that wasn't earlier? About the time the light got brighter?"

"No," said Campbell. "Definitely no. There was no one about —except me in my bush—until the struggle on the ladder was well in train. Why?"

"Tell you presently. Please go on."

"The dark figure cantered along and apparently ran into the ladder, which fell down, leaving your visitor swinging. The next second he dropped, too, almost on top of the other man. There was a flash and a crack; one man fell down and the other ran away. I don't know where he went; I was taken by surprise, I suppose. Actually, I was watching the man on the ground, to see if he were moving at all. He wasn't. I don't even know who shot which or which man ran away, it was all such a mix-up and happened so quickly. Well, after that lights came on and people began to arrive, so I went off and picked flowers. End of story."

"The manager told me," said Hambledon, "that he came out for a breath of fresh air before retiring and saw a ladder at my window. So he rushed back indoors and got the night porter and they both came up to my room. I know that's true. It was their arrival that started the uproar; they arrived just before the light went out."

"There was nobody about here after the ladder was put up until the last moment, as I've told you," said Campbell, "but I suppose he might easily have just peered round the corner and dodged back without my seeing him."

"I expect that's what happened," said Hambledon. "I can't see Lacroix sticking his little golden head into anything that looks like trouble."

"Did you say he was drinking brandy?" asked Forgan. "He must have been upset, poor little shrinking violet. Normally he drinks orange juice. I asked him once whether he had a conscientious objection to alcohol, but he said not conscientious. He avoided it because, he said, it coarsened the skin. Then he glanced casually at mine, but that may have been unintentional."

"You gave him the benefit of the doubt," said Campbell, "since he is still alive?"

"I did, yes. I had not my butterfly net with me. Oh, Hambledon, have you seen our detective from Orleans? Lean and beaky and rolls his own cigarettes. He came this evening."

"Have I?" said Hambledon vaguely. "I don't know. The place is full of strangers. Well, if that's all for the moment, I'd better get back to my room in case anyone comes to look for me. Oh, by the way, I haven't yet told you what happened to me. Strong light shining in my eyes, couldn't see a thing. Porter came in, light went out, intruder went out, porter and I went out. End of story, if I have your permission to quote you, Campbell. The intruder was looking for something of Power's. I don't think he found it. Perhaps I shall. See you tomorrow or, to be more accurate, later today. Oh, by the way, have you noticed the telephones? Completely automatic, you just dial the room number and there you are."

"We had noticed them," said Forgan, "but we had no one we particularly wished to talk to except Power, and he warned us not to use them. At least, not to talk to him. We use them daily to address the dining-room on the subject of the menu; they work very well."

"They must have cost something to install," said Hambledon.

"But so convenient to be able to ring up another room at any hour of the day or night," said Campbell. "The French think of everything, don't they?"

Hambledon laughed. "But I agree with Power; we'd better not use them between ourselves. Well, good night."

Hambledon returned to his room just in time; he had hardly closed the door when there came a knock upon it.

"*Entrez!*"

The door opened and a man entered, lean and beaky as Forgan had said, with a pleasant smile.

"Excuse me, please. Detective Sergeant Vidal of Orleans. It is my duty to inform you that there will be an enquiry into the death here tonight of Raoul Rougisson of Paris. The Juge d'Instruction will hold the enquiry here at ten o'clock tomorrow morning and you are asked not to leave these premises, if you please, until it is over. That is understood?"

"Certainly it is and I promise that I will not abscond."

"Monsieur is English," said Vidal apologetically. "I was not sure whether he was familiar with our procedure. I wish Monsieur a good night." He went out, and the door closed behind him.

"In that case," said Tommy, "bed, thank goodness."

The enquiry was held by the same Juge d'Instruction who had presided over the Power enquiry held on the previous day. He said so himself.

"Seldom can it occur, in a small and peaceful rural community such as Arnage-sur-Loire, that two——" and so on.

The witnesses, to the number of seventy-nine, moved uneasily upon chairs brought in from all parts of the hotel to replace small tables hurriedly carried out of the dining-room, while at a long trestle table down one side of the room, reporters shifted and whispered together.

"First of all," said the Juge, "evidence of identity."

The Orleans Superintendent of Police stood up and said that as the deceased had not formerly been known by anyone in Arnage, it was thought advisable to have the identification made by someone who knew him personally. It had not been possible in so short a time to get in touch with Madame Rougisson, who was away from her flat for the night, but the police were greatly under an obligation to Monsieur Henri Delamere for kindly volunteering to give evidence of identity. Monsieur Henri Delamere.

An ancient round-shouldered figure rose unsteadily from the front row. He had long grey hair which trickled over his collar, a white puffy face, and red-rimmed eyes which peered rather than looked about him. He had a pair of thick-lensed glasses in his hand which he continually put on and took off again as though they did not make much difference one way or the other but there was always the hope. The Juge took one look at him and courteously begged him to give his evidence sitting.

"Thank you," said the witness. He turned and felt rather vaguely for the back of his chair, set it carefully behind his knees, and sat down. Hambledon wondered whether this man could rightly be described as an eyewitness, but that was the Juge's responsibility.

"Henri Delamere, is it a fact that the deceased Raoul Rougisson was known to you personally?"

"Certainly. Over a period of years we have been corresponding from time to time over matters of joint ornithological and entomological interest. I am an entomologist; that is, I study insects, beetles, and so forth. He was an ornithologist; that is, he studied birds. Since a large proportion of our bird population is insectivorous, I hope it will be plain that our interests and observations overlapped to quite a large extent."

"Thank you, yes," said the Juge. "But you say you corresponded with him. May I know whether you in fact knew him personally—were you in the habit of meeting him as well as writing to him?"

"Yes, yes. Dear me, yes. I met him several times at scientific gatherings; also, he came to my house once or twice. Yes, of course I knew him perfectly well. But I want to lodge a very emphatic protest at having been——"

"May we have your protest later, please? If you would kindly answer my questions first. Did you this morning see a body in the mortuary here in——"

"But that is what I wish to protest about! I heard in Orleans— I live there—that Rougisson had been murdered last night, and it seemed to me so absurd a story that I went to the police to ask if it were true. Before I could say a word I was gathered in by that type of a superintendent there, pushed into a car, whirled out here, and thrust into a dank outhouse where was a dead body on a stone slab! I detest dead bodies. The sheet was pulled back and I was imperiously urged to look at it! An outrage! I protest with all the vehemence of which I am capable! I am Henri Delamere, not an undertaker——"

"At the moment," interrupted the Juge, "you are Henri Delamere, a witness on oath for the information of the Procureur de la République in a——"

"Nor a necrophilist either," raged the ancient, and the Superintendent rose in his place to deny that any discourtesy whatever, let alone force, had been used——

"Be quiet, Superintendent," said the Juge testily. "You, Delamere, did you or did you not see a body in the mortuary this morning?"

"Yes," said the old man sulkily.

"And did you recognize it?"

"Yes, of course I did."

"Whose body was it?"

"Good gracious, have you not grasped yet that it was Rougisson's?"

"Raoul Rougisson, the ornithologist?"

"Permit me to offer my felicitations," said Delamere acidly. "Monsieur travels slowly but he arrives at last."

"Next witness!"

"Have I your leave to go? I suppose it is necessary to ask your leave," said Delamere.

"It is. You may go at once."

The old man got up and blundered out of the room, angrily shaking off the guiding hand of one of the police. The Juge raised his eyes to heaven, and one or two people tittered.

When decorum had been restored, the Juge d'Instruction called upon every person present to say whether or not they had seen or heard anything and, if so, what. This performance did not take so long as one might expect, Gallet acting as master of ceremonies with a list in his hand.

"Monsieur Aristide Quennellet," he said, and a stout elderly Frenchman rose to his feet.

"Aristide Quennellet," said the Juge d'Instruction, "where were you at ten minutes past two this morning?"

"Asleep in my bed, if you please."

"And your room number is——?"

"Forty-seven, on the second floor."

Gallet nodded.

"In relation to Room 31, where is your room situated?"

"Diametrically opposite, as you might say, back to back with the whole hotel between. And one floor higher."

The Juge referred to a plan on his table and nodded.

"Quennellet, did you hear or see anything whatever between, say, half-past one and twenty minutes past two?"

"Nothing whatever. I was asleep before midnight and did not wake until I was called this morning."

"Thank you. Next witness."

Very few had heard anything at that time, fewer still had seen anything; in fact, only three. Most of those who had awakened in the night had done so when people "began galloping in the passages and talking," as one elderly lady put it.

"What did you do then, madame?"

"Nothing."

"You did not get out of bed to look out of the door or the window?"

"Neither."

"You are not curious to know the reason if people are about in the small hours?"

"Monsieur, I was far too well brought up."

"Next witness."

Hambledon's evidence was long and he was fully questioned.

"You can give us no clue at all as to the identity of the intruder?"

"None, monsieur. I never saw him."

"His voice?"

"He never spoke above a whisper. He had no particular accent. I would say well educated."

The night porter. "Not a big man, monsieur, but strong. I never saw his face, but he had a beard. A short stiff beard. I felt it; it touched my hand."

Lacroix, the manager. He saw the ladder, warned the porter, and went with him to the door of Room 31. Did not enter. When the door was opened he went away.

"Where to?"

"Downstairs, Monsieur le Juge. Into the lounge."

"And then?"

"I sat down. I was feeling ill. I had fluctuations in the stomach, tremblings in the limbs, and a nervous headache."

"So you just continued to sit? You saw and heard nothing?"

"I heard the crack of the gun, Monsieur le Juge. I heard it through an adjacent window, I suppose. It was outside."

"What did you do then?"

"I became faint. I poured myself a little brandy for restorative purposes. I was still sipping it when Monsieur Hambledon and the porter came running down the stairs. They passed me and went outside."

"You did not accompany them?"

"Oh no, no. I am afflicted with a sensitive nature, I cannot bear violence or the sight of blood."

The Juge raised his eyebrows and changed the subject.

"The deceased, Raoul Rougisson, you knew him?"

"He had been staying here for a little over a week, Monsieur le Juge. I did not know him before that, but he is a well-known man, a member of various learned societies. The reference books tell——"

"The police also have access to reference books, Lacroix. What did he do while he was here?"

"He was out most days, with his binoculars, counting the birds, or so he told me. At night, too, for the owls. I understand that he informed the porter when he would be out late."

"*Counting* the birds?"

"He told me that he was making a quantitative survey of the birds of the Loire Valley."

"Next witness."

Gallet, the undermanager; followed by such of the hotel servants as lived on the premises. No further detail came to light, and the Juge d'Instruction, for the second time in two days, declared that a murder had been committed in Arnage-sur-Loire and that the police would proceed with their investigations to elucidate the mystery. Detective Sergeant Vidal, sitting in a corner watching everyone, saying nothing and making a note occasionally, looked modestly down his nose and continued to say nothing.

CHAPTER 6   *The Nobleman*

AFTER LUNCH Hambledon went to Orleans, called
upon the Superintendent of Police there, and presented his cre-
dentials. Mutual confidence having been established, Hambledon
said that he had been sent out by his government to look into
the death of Alan Power just to make sure that everything was
all right, as it were. Monsieur le Surintendant was probably painfully aware of the tendency of governments to fuss, though in
this case they seemed to have something to fuss about since it
now appeared that the poor young man had been murdered. He
then leaned back in his chair, accepted a cigarette, and beamed
upon the Superintendent.

The Superintendent said yes, yes indeed, all that was perfectly
true, and the tendency of governments to fuss was plainly an
occupational disease which periodically attacked all governments
alike, regardless of politics, nationality, or even colour. He then
insisted upon Hambledon's having a glass of wine and paused in
the act of pouring it out to say: "Nonetheless, this is the first time
in my experience that the English Government has sent out a
special emissary to enquire into the death of a young Englishman in a road accident."

He filled the glass and his own, and they drank to each other
in the customary manner.

"I believe that to be the case," said Tommy blandly.

"Looking at your card," said the Superintendent, taking it up,
"I see that you are on the staff of the Foreign Office. Do I gather
from that that Monsieur Power was admittedly a man of some
importance? I stress the word 'admittedly.' "

Hambledon put down his glass and laughed. "I was only trying, monsieur, in my tactless, blundering manner, to find out

whether you were interested in this affair as it really is or whether you preferred to treat it as a plain murder, a matter for your police, and nothing more. Because, although I should be more than thankful for your collaboration, I have no shadow of right to expect it."

The Superintendent smiled.

"Monsieur Power was not unknown to me, though I never met him," he said. "The Paris police told me about him and that he was on the track of these damned people. You knew that, of course. They murdered a financier in Paris early this year, and his death started the slide in television shares, which finally broke the bank in Monaco. You know about that, of course."

"The bank collapse was in all the papers, naturally, but I did not know what had originally set it off."

"Monsieur Power was working with the Paris police on that murder. It seems that they liked him, because I have received over the telephone the most horrible threats of what will happen to me if I do not find his murderer. From men some of whom have been my friends for years; notably one Antoine Letord." The Superintendent cocked one eye at Hambledon.

"He is a friend of mine too; I have known him for a number of years, ever since he held me up at the point of a gun in Brussels soon after the war."

The Superintendent chuckled. "He did not tell me that, but I am not surprised. He and I were at school together and he was always impulsive. Perhaps that is why he is now near the top of the tree at the Sûreté while I am but a policeman in the provinces. But you see, Monsieur Hambledon, how things come about. A young man drives too fast and his car goes off the road and he is killed. Very sad for his relations, but it happens so often, does it not? Then it appears that he is a friend of the Sûreté, he is also one of your so justly famous MI 5, yes? At once the news comes that he is not merely dead, he is murdered. But in the morning before I hear that news I have a telephone call from Letord. 'My old friend Hambledon of British Intelligence is on his way to Arnage. What is the truth about Power? If you do not assist Hambledon by all possible means I will wring both your ears off.' So impulsive, Letord."

"I can just hear him saying it!"

"So when an information is laid to the police that Power has a bullet in the head, I go to the enquiry, I myself. A queer type, that Rougisson, eh? I assume that was true, about his seeing the birds fly up. They would, you know. I was——"

"It wasn't," said Tommy. "It was a thundering lie, for he was in a tobacconist's shop in the village buying cigarettes when it happened." He repeated what the woman in the shop had told him.

"Then how the devil did he know that there was a shot fired? Can you tell me that?"

"I have not the dimmest outline of an idea," said Hambledon.

"Nor I. Because, you see, it is not in character. Definitely not. This Raoul Rougisson, he was a distinguished ornithologist and very well known. I read an article of his in one of the weeklies only the other day, and about a month ago he gave a talk about birds on the radio and I heard it. Most interesting, monsieur, fascinating. When, therefore, he said he knew a shot had been fired because of the way the birds flew up, I believed him at once. It had the authentic air, you know? Yes. Now you come and tell me that that was a lie because he was in a village shop buying cigarettes while the affair was happening three kilometres away. Are you perfectly certain that the woman was not talking about some previous occasion when she and Rougisson stood together in the shop and watched Power drive past?"

"All I can say is that she said so. Probably some confirmation could——"

"I will put Maroche on to it. Maroche looks slow but he is nobody's fool, Monsieur Hambledon, and he knows his people as I know my own family. I will ring him up. Let me refill your glass. Now then."

The Superintendent was put through to the police station at Arnage, and by good fortune Maroche was there. His Chief set out the case and added: "You see the point. Could it have been some other day? Or earlier that day?"

"Not earlier that day, for Monsieur Power could not get his car out for over an hour, and even then it was still early. The shop would not have been open more than an hour earlier. No. The previous day—is it permitted that I consider?"

"Certainly," said the Superintendent, and put his hand over the mouthpiece. "He always says that—'is it permitted that I consider?'—and then one waits while the machinery revolves. I tell you, I have—— Yes, Maroche, what is it?"

"Monsieur Power died on Thursday. He came here on Tuesday night late, I saw him arrive. The day between, Wednesday, Madame Grosset was away at Sens all day for the marriage of her niece who used to live with her, Marcelle Nivot. The daughter of the postmistress here kept shop for Madame Grosset all that day. Before that, Monsieur Power had not been here for some three weeks, and Monsieur Rougisson only came nine days ago. So, if you please, it seems it must have been that Thursday morning."

"Yes, I see. Maroche! Not a hint of that is to get out. Do not even ask for corroboration."

"It is understood, mon Surintendant."

The Superintendent repeated the gist of this to Hambledon. "So you were quite right and we are no further on."

"I had much rather have been wrong," said Hambledon.

"I repeat, it does not fit," said the Frenchman gloomily. "How could he have known? Or has he, also, this birdwatcher, a finger in the pie of these financial swindles?"

"A finger against them, surely, since he gave the information."

"It is true. And now he is dead also, so we cannot ask him. May ten thousand devils torment the man who killed him! I suppose his death was mere coincidence; he happened to come along?"

"I suppose so too. But the man in my room was searching for something he thought Power might have hidden there."

"Do you think," said the Frenchman, "that Rougisson knew that and was trying to take it from him, whatever it might be?"

Hambledon shook his head. "I don't know at all."

"By the way, Monsieur Power rang me up just before he started that morning. He said he was coming in to see me and had something to show me——"

"Yes indeed, and that was one of my reasons for coming to see you today." Hambledon took out his wallet and gave the Superintendent the little square of glossy picture postcard which had been in Power's notebook. "There's a fingerprint on it, as you see. Power though it the same as one the police found when your

59

murdered financier's flat was ransacked in Paris. He found this in a stand of postcards for sale on the reception desk at the Hotel de la Poste at Arnage. He wanted it checked."

"I will see to it myself." The Frenchman wrote on an envelope, slipped the piece of card inside, and looked at Hambledon. "Since this was before you arrived at Arnage, would it be tactless of me to ask how you know about it?"

Hambledon explained how Power had asked for assistants not from the department and how Forgan and Campbell had come out to him. "You saw one of them at the enquiry, the Dr. Farelli with a Spanish accent. He's the Englishman Forgan."

"But I thought he had a mental patient—what has become of the other——?"

"He's the mental patient. You see," as the Superintendent's eyes and mouth opened, "if you are a little—er—mentally unstable no one queries anything you do. Do they?"

The Frenchman shook with laughter. "It's a good cover, certainly, I must meet him sometime."

"Don't offer him an orange," advised Hambledon.

"Speaking seriously. They saw the crash, yes? And then went through Power's pockets while the lorry driver went for the police. Yes, I see. And examined Power's head, too, no doubt, which accounts for the promptitude with which Monsieur Hambledon comes on the scene? Good, very good. Anything else?"

"They also found this." Hambledon laid an expended .22 cartridge case on the desk. "They found that up in the bushes where the murderer had lain in wait. Your Constable Maroche also found the spot later."

"I will have this looked into; it will probably be a help. We are testing the local guns, as you know, I expect. That is, the ballistics experts in Paris are doing so, and I will send them this also. You have one of our best men at Arnage in Detective Sergeant Vidal. I sent him out on the Power case, of course; now he can look into the other as well. Are they one case, Monsieur Hambledon, or two?"

"I seem to have spent most of this interview saying 'I don't know' to every question you ask, and now I must say it again. There is another thing which strikes me as needlessly mysterious: the mortuary being broken into."

60

"So we thought, so we fingerprinted it and got a nice set of prints. We even know whose they are—one Polydore d'Aquitaine."

"Who is the nobleman?"

"An elderly tramp. It is said that he was an actor when he was young and that was his stage name. He is a harmless nuisance; he wanders about these central provinces of France sleeping rough and pilfering, usually only food, but occasionally a little loose money, an old coat or a pair of boots, no more. He has never been known to offer violence to any or to engage in brawls even with his own kind. We in Orleans have had him through our hands several times, so we had his prints on record. He creeps round villages at night; if he finds an unfastened window he slips in, but he seldom goes beyond the first room he enters and he never takes anything valuable; only food, as I said, and a little small change. We are looking for him now; he will be picked up easily enough."

"But why should such as he break into a mortuary?"

"Did he know it was one, monsieur? He may have been looking for somewhere to sleep. An unoccupied building, sound and weatherproof——"

"Only it was not unoccupied. He must have had a shock if he turned back the sheet," said Hambledon.

"Yes. Somebody had turned back the sheet and scattered the flowers, had they not? I think he replaced it hastily and fled, for there were some good clothes there and they had not been touched. Poor old Polydore! Still, we will have him in and talk to him, though I do not suppose it will take us any further. It is but to knit in that loose end."

"Just so. I am more grateful than I can say, Monsieur le Surintendant, for being allowed to sit here with you and talk the matter out as we have done. One kindness more, would you have the goodness to recommend me to the good offices of Detective Sergeant Vidal?"

"With the greatest pleasure. I will write to him and the letter shall go tonight. Is there anything more before we part for the time?"

"Nothing, thank you. I was just wondering what sort of gun was used to shoot Rougisson."

"We shall know tonight. The autopsy is being performed this

evening, and I will see that you have the result. It will be interesting if that is a point two-two also, will it not?"

Hambledon travelled back to Arnage, thinking as he went that the first thing he would do upon arrival was to search his own bedroom. If Power had left anything hidden there it was unlikely that the intruder had found it since he was still searching when the night porter burst in. The police had gone over the room for fingerprints while the enquiry was in progress; after that there had been housemaids scurrying to catch up with the two hours' delay in the daily routine. Hambledon was not anxious; later in the day would do very well for his search; the hiding place would not be obvious, and he wanted some undisturbed time to look thoroughly for it.

He went straight up to his room, pulled open a drawer for a clean handkerchief, and stopped abruptly. Like most men who travel much and have to wait upon themselves, Hambledon was neat and methodical in the disposal of his clothes and personal gear. Handkerchiefs and collars in one drawer, socks and ties in another, shirts and pyjamas, and so on, sorted and tidily stacked. They were not now; they had been snatched up and flung back by someone in haste. The paper covering the bottoms of the drawers had been dragged up and pushed back crookedly.

"Most interesting," said Tommy in a pleased voice. "The thing was not found last night, so another search has been made. By broad daylight, in the middle of the afternoon, the intruder came back and had another go. I say the intruder came back because I suppose so; it's more reasonable than that several different men should queue up to take turns at searching my room. Someone who walked through the hotel without being challenged, which rather suggests someone staying in the hotel. This is an interesting case, it is really. Of course the police went through the room this morning. Did I open a drawer after they had gone? No, I didn't. But they wouldn't hurl my things about, or would they? I'll ask Vidal."

Hambledon hunted round the room and looked in all the places where long experience had taught him to look, but he found nothing and was not surprised. Either there had never been anything to find or it had been found already.

CHAPTER 7   *One Knife, One Fork, One Spoon*

ON THE following morning Hambledon, coming
out of his bedroom, met Vidal in the corridor. Since it was the
hour of breakfast, most people were in their rooms with coffee
and rolls or in the dining-room with coffee and rolls, and the
housemaids had not yet started their morning gallop. The corridor was for the moment empty, and Hambledon took advantage
of it.

"Monsieur Vidal? Could you spare me a moment?"

"Certainly, monsieur," said Vidal, "any number of moments."

"Come into my room, will you?"

When the door was shut Vidal said: "I have heard this morning
from my Chief in Orleans that Monsieur and I are colleagues.
It is an honour for me and I will do my best to live up to it."

Hambledon laughed. "I have done little so far but answer 'I
do not know' to every question your Chief asked me, but I study
to improve. Tell me, your men searched this room yesterday during the enquiry, did they?"

"I searched it myself, monsieur, while you were having breakfast, and found nothing, not even a fingerprint. The large electric
torch which was here was not yours, was it? I understood your
visitor left it."

"That is so, and I hope it will help you."

"Not it," said Vidal cheerfully. "There are thousands like it all
over France. But, I beg Monsieur's pardon, you were going to
say something?"

"When you searched, did you go through my drawers also?"

"But, no——"

"Look. Someone did." Hambledon pulled out the drawers to
show him. "I left them for you to see."

63

"When was this done, do you know?"

"I think, yesterday afternoon when I was in Orleans."

"He did not find what he wanted in the night so he came back in the afternoon?" said Vidal.

"I assume so."

"Someone whose presence in the corridors occasioned no remark. I wonder if he found it."

"He may have done so," said Hambledon. "There was something else I was going to say. When Rougisson was killed, the porter and I came up with a torch, and the dead man was wearing gloves. I don't know why it struck me so, but it did. To die with your boots on, well and good, but not gloves. It isn't right."

"Too domestic and homely? I agree with Monsieur. I noticed that myself, but it seems that Monsieur Rougisson always wore them when he went out at night. He would stand by the porter's desk talking to him and pulling them on. When the porter made some comment Monsieur said it was for the thorns. One cannot see brambles in the dark."

"Quite simple when it is explained!"

"Most things are, monsieur, it is but to find the explanation. I have two pieces of news for Monsieur. One, the bullet that killed Rougisson was a nine-millimetre. Two, that Polydore the tramp has been picked up and is now on his way to Orleans, so my Superintendent can knit in that loose end. My Chief, he always knits in the loose end. We all have our favourite phrases, do we not?"

"One more thing I must tell you if your Chief did not. My two assistants—no? Well, they are the Spanish Dr. Farelli and his mentally disturbed patient."

"And his patient? He who sat upon the lawn early this morning making daisy chains? Surely not."

"Even so. They are both English and I believe you will find them helpful."

"I have no words," said Vidal simply. "What a cover!"

"I hear the pails of housemaids," said Hambledon. "I go."

Polydore d'Aquitaine, shrinking and sagging at the knees, was brought before the Superintendent at Orleans, who looked him up and down with a grim smile. There were also present Detective Sergeant Vidal and Police Constable Maroche.

"You are an old nuisance, Polydore, and have been for years, but this is too much. You have overstepped yourself this time."

"May I know," said the tramp, drawing himself up, "what I am alleged to have done this time?" He had a deep and resonant voice, most unexpected from such a scarecrow figure, and his diction was excellent if a little overemphasized. As was said by a party of British hikers who encountered him: "At any moment you expect him to say: 'Laddie, when I played Hamlet——'"

"Pinching loaves through cottage windows is bad enough, but breaking into a mortuary——"

Polydore leapt as though someone had stuck a pin into him and began to tremble.

"No, no. Never. I never did, I never would. I cannot endure to be near the dead. Once, when I was young—— May I sit down?"

"Give him a chair."

"Not the dead, I can't bear it. Thank you for your kindness to an old man broken by years and sorrow. No, Monsieur le Surintendant. I cannot even pass a funeral, I must turn off another way. To look at that box and think what is inside——" He shuddered.

"If your face were cleaner," said the Superintendent, not unkindly, "I should say you had turned green, but it won't do, Polydore. At Arnage-sur-Loire, on the night of——"

"I do not know the place. I have never visited it. I do not even know where it is."

"It will not do, Polydore. On the night of Thursday last, the mortuary at Arnage was broken into——"

"I was not anywhere near——"

"And your fingerprints were found on the window sill."

Polydore d'Aquitaine sank and settled in his chair till he looked like a heap of rags with a discreditable grey head insecurely balanced on the top, and there was a long pause.

"Well?" said the Superintendent eventually. "Are you going to talk?"

"I have been trying to forget it, but you have forced it back into my mind." The tramp straightened up. "I was at Arnage that night and I will now tell you a dreadful story."

"Not a story, Polydore. The truth."

"It will be the truth. To cleanse my bosom of this perilous stuff——"

"And that's the first time I have ever known you to ask for a bath. Get on."

"I came into Arnage as the evening light was fading into shadows and darkness, and one by one the candles in cottage windows were put out."

"In other words, you hung about till everyone had gone to bed."

"I wandered round the village looking in dustbins for a mouldy crust——"

"Maroche?"

"Half a loaf and a piece of cheese from the Widow Lassalle, mon Surintendant, and the cobbler thinks he lost some onions, number unknown."

"Go on, Polydore."

"I found something to eat, the first food to have passed my lips that day, and I looked for somewhere retired to enjoy it. There was a building by itself, a little back from the road, a poor small place with no lights in its two windows. I went round behind it and found a bank to sit upon. All this, messieurs, which seems misery to you, was luxury to me. I sat down and began to eat, slowly and thankfully. Suddenly I heard footsteps and I shrank back." Polydore d'Aquitaine, actor, shrank back in his seat and held up trembling hands to ward off some threat of danger. "The footsteps came up to the building and stopped. I could see nothing, for I was behind it, the corner parted us from each other. I waited, holding my breath. There was a faint scratching noise, a click, and then the sound of a window being cautiously raised." The narrator leaned forward, his face alight with interest and one hand cupped behind his ear. "I listened intently and heard a scrambling noise as of someone climbing in. I am curious, messieurs, I admit it; I have always been curious, and life itself has not cured me of that vice. I rose silently to my feet"—he did so—"advanced to the corner and peered round it." He mimed someone peering round a wall until Maroche almost believed there must be a wall there. "What did I see? Nothing and nobody."

"You know," said the Superintendent, addressing Vidal, "no one can deny that this man can tell a story. Were you here when he was found with his head stuck in a window at Tigny? The sash cord broke and let the sash down on the back of his neck, and there he had to stay till somebody released him. When they asked him what he was doing there he said he had heard a child crying and was singing to it to lull it to sleep. Well, Polydore? You saw nothing and nobody because there was no one else there, is that it?"

"No, monsieur. I crept round far enough to see that the window was open at the bottom; I crept on till I could see there was a light in the place, a moving light. A few steps further and I could see in at the window. There was a man in there with an electric torch in his hand; he was standing by a table in the middle which was covered with some white stuff. The light was reflected up from this and I could see him quite well. Then he tucked the torch under one armpit, to leave his hands free, as I suppose. He stretched out a gloved hand and stripped back the white covering ——messieurs, under it was a naked corpse!" Polydore closed his eyes and shuddered violently. "I have told you I cannot bear to look on the dead. My knees gave way; my hands, as it were, froze themselves to the window sill. I closed my eyes and said a prayer I learned at my mother's knee. When I opened them again this man was turning the corpse over on its side; it came over all in one piece like a wooden doll. He held it like that with one arm, directing the torch upon the head; with the other hand he was searching and feeling through the thick hair."

Polydore's long fingers, grimed with dirt but still shapely and expressive, mimed the circling motions.

"I could bear it no longer—I tore my hands from the window sill and fled away from that dreadful place. Staggering and stumbling in the dark"—he ranged round the charge room with eyes wide open and hands weaving before him while the interested police got out of his way—"sometimes falling; I rushed away from that accursed spot for ever. Never, never again will I approach within ten kilometres of Arnage-sur-Loire, where men disturb the dead at midnight for their own foul purposes."

Polydore stopped, drew himself up, strode back to his chair, and sat down upon it with dignity and decision.

"That, Monsieur le Surintendant is my story, every word of which is the bitter truth."

"Splendid. In fact, magnificent. I congratulate you from the bottom of my heart. This man whom you say you saw inside the mortuary, what was he like?"

"Of medium height," said Polydore, frowning in thought, "and medium build. Neither stout nor slim. I could not tell the colour of his hair, but it was thick and bushy. He had also a short bristling beard. His face was unremarkable, but it was not a young face—a man in the fifties, as I should judge. He wore no glasses but he did wear gloves, brown ones. I could not see his clothes, for he wore a raincoat over them. I could not tell the colour. That is all I can tell you, messieurs."

"I see. Thank you very much. Now you——"

"I can go now?"

"Go? Certainly not," said the Superintendent. "You are going in the cells, of course, what did you think?"

"In the cells! Why? Upon what charge?"

"Of breaking into the mortuary at Arn——"

"But I did not! I have told you precisely what happened!"

"I know you did, but did you seriously suppose that we believed that rigmarole? Sing the baby to sleep!"

"If at other times," said Polydore earnestly, "I have sometimes endeavoured to put a favourable complexion upon a set of awkward circumstances, I assure you that this time at least I am telling the exact truth. Can it really be that you do not believe me?"

"It can. We are in your debt for half an hour of most excellent entertainment, but we don't believe a word of it."

"You are wrong, monsieur, completely wrong——"

"Take him away."

Polydore was removed, moaning and protesting, to a cell where he was searched and his grubby possessions gingerly routed out from the recesses of his clothes. They were listed in detail, put into a cardboard box, and removed. The cell door closed and the key turned in the lock.

He sat down on the bed and took his head in his hands. He hated being in jail; the mere thought of a door locked upon him made him feel ill. Besides, this crime might be serious, much worse than a little harmless pilfering. If only there were some means of convincing these hardhearted police of the truth of his

68

story. If only he had a cigarette. They had taken away his little tin box which held quite a useful number of cigarette stubs and an even greater treasure, nearly half a cigar. And—and something else——

He sprang to his feet and began to hammer on the door.

"What," said the Superintendent, "did you think of that?"

"Not quite his usual," said one of his sergeants. "I mean, so much of it."

"Something he said," said Vidal, "put me in mind of something, but I don't know what. A—I know. His description of that man. If he'd been making it up it would have been more striking, would it not? Medium this, medium that, bushy hair and bristling beard——"

His Chief shot out a finger. "You're thinking of Rougisson."

Vidal stared. "That may be. I——"

A gendarme came in. "By permission. The prisoner is banging on the door, demanding to see Monsieur le Surintendant. Says he's just remembered something he had forgotten. Says it is very important."

"The only thing which struck me," said the Superintendent, "was his persisting like that. Generally he tells some tale and we all laugh and he shrugs his shoulders and goes inside. None of this 'but it is true.' Shall we have him back? Bring him in."

Polydore returned.

"Among my things which were rudely taken from me," he began, "there is a small tin box."

"Containing," corroborated the gendarme, "cigarette stubs."

"If you have bluffed your way back here," said the Superintendent, "merely because you want a smoke——"

Polydore lifted his hand.

"Certainly not," he said. "I know the rules in these places as well as you do. In that box, besides the cigarette ends, there is a button with a strip of cloth attached, as though it had been roughly torn from a garment." Vidal threw up his head, but Polydore swept on. "I remember now. When I clung to that window sill I felt a button under my fingers; when I ran away I was clasping it still. It might have been that the man who got in caught it on the sill and wrenched it off. I all but hurled from me

69

the memento of a ghastly experience," said Polydore dramatically, "but when one is as poor as I, a button is still a button. It is in my tin box; look for yourselves, you who say I lie."

The tin box was produced and the button taken out. Attached to it was a thin strip of grey proofed material such as is used for raincoats. Vidal took it and examined it, and his Chief watched his face.

"Take him back," said the Superintendent to the gendarme, and Polydore swaggered back to the cell as one doing the company a favour. "Well, Vidal?"

Vidal looked up. "There was a button missing from Rougisson's raincoat," he said slowly, "and a strip torn down like this. We assumed that it had been torn off in the struggle when he was shot. We have that coat here, mon Surintendant——"

The Superintendent turned to the station sergeant.

"Bring it here."

When it was brought and laid upon the desk, Polydore's button matched all the others and the torn strip fitted to a thread the rent in the cloth from which it had been torn.

"That is conclusive," said Vidal. "It was Rougisson who broke into the mortuary. It also explains how he knew that Power had been shot."

"But why, why?" demanded his Chief, banging the desk. "Why did he break in, why examine the head? He must have had some reason. Rougisson the ornithologist, the birdwatcher, the writer of scientific articles, the member of learned societies, the lecturer upon the radio, why is he running about like an amateur detective in a *roman policier* solving murder mysteries? It does not fit. As I said to the English Monsieur Hambledon, it does not fit."

There was a short silence, eventually broken by Maroche, who said that perhaps it was, as one might say, deceased's hobby, as it were. The Superintendent emitted a sizzling sound between his teeth, and Vidal intervened to ask what was to be done about Polydore. "For it appears that he has, for once, told us the truth."

"Yes. More than that, he has helped us. I think we must let him go; we've got nothing against him now."

Police Constable Maroche cleared his throat and remarked diffidently that there was, after all, the little matter of the Widow Lassalle's loaf and cheese and the onions of the cobbler.

"Phoo," said his Chief, waving away both widow and cobbler. "Serves the woman right for not shutting her larder window. Bring the fellow in again, Sergeant."

So Polydore d'Aquitaine once more entered the charge room, sauntering gracefully, pointing his toes, bowing to the company, and dusting the tips of his fingers together, straight out of *Le Bourgeois Gentilhomme* at the Comédie Française.

"Well, you old mountebank," said the Superintendent genially, "we have decided to let you off this time."

"Justice always prevails, except when deliberately perverted," said Polydore blandly.

"I think you're being rude. Never mind. Give him back his things, Sergeant. And here, Polydore. Here's something for you." The Superintendent gave him an unopened packet of Gauloise Bleue cigarettes. "Have you any matches? Here's a box for you also. Sergeant, he is to have a meal before he goes. Not in the cell, he is not a prisoner; serve it somewhere else. Au 'voir, Polydore. Be good and keep out of my clutches for the future."

"I thank Monsieur for his bounty to a poor old man. But this is not au revoir, it is adieu, unless Monsieur is shifted to another post, for I am leaving this district at once for ever, and Orleans will see my face no more."

"Orleans will bear up. Take him away, Sergeant." When Polydore had completed an effective exit, the Superintendent said that he had always had a soft spot for that old rogue.

The sergeant took the tramp to his own house, entering by the back door and stopping him in the scullery.

"Wait here, I'll get you a chair, and the wife will let you have a meal."

The sergeant came back in a moment with a wooden chair, and his wife followed after with a plate of stew and vegetables. She wrinkled her nose when she saw their guest, but made no comment and went back into the kitchen.

"There you are," said the sergeant, peeling off his coat and hanging it up from habit on the back of the door. "Eat that and be thankful when it should have been prison diet if you'd had your deserts. How you get away with it I do not know. One knife, one fork, one spoon," he added pointedly. "And one plate, too, of course."

He went into the kitchen for his own meal and his wife told him to shut the intervening door; she had, she said, a sensitive nose that was easily affronted, especially at mealtimes. Polydore said nothing, but his eyes gleamed.

A quarter of an hour later the sergeant returned and found his guest polishing an already clean plate with a piece of bread. He rose to his feet.

"One knife, one spoon, one fork," he said, pointing them out. "And one plate, of course. May I speak to your good lady a moment?"

The sergeant's wife put her head in at the door.

"Madame, your husband is a fortunate and happy man. Your cooking is like that of the little angels in Paradise; your stew is such as is served upon silver dishes at the Tour d'Argent in Paris."

"Enchanted," she said, and vanished again as Polydore took up his hat and the sergeant opened the back door for him.

"Now hop it," said the sergeant, "and don't let me see you in these parts again."

"My good man, may all your wishes be as easily granted. Adieu."

Polydore walked off up the road, and the sergeant's eyes followed him as he turned in at the entrance to the Orleans railway station.

"Looking round for something to pick up. He'll be back," prophesied the sergeant.

Later that afternoon the Sergeant, being off duty, turned in to his favourite *estaminet* for a glass of wine and there met a friend who was a booking clerk at the railway station. The clerk stood the sergeant one and the sergeant returned the hospitality, or meant to do so. He put his hand into his coat pocket and found it empty.

"What—I had some money here, I know I had."

"Lost it? Was there much? Perhaps you've got a slit in the pocket."

"I have not. Two hundred and fifty francs."

"You've left it at home," said the clerk. "That's funny, that's the same amount. I had the most awful old scarecrow of a tramp you ever saw come up to my *quichet* today and lay down that exact sum. He wanted a single for as far south as that money would take him."

"Oh," said the sergeant feebly. "Did you serve him?"

"Of course. And gave him three francs change."

The sergeant had occasion, when he returned to duty, to enter the office of the Superintendent, who looked up.

"Did Polydore go off all right, Sergeant?"

"Yes, mon Surintendant."

"He's an old rascal, but one can't help liking him."

The sergeant did not answer.

HAMBLEDON WENT to Paris to see his old friend Antoine Letord, now holding a rank equivalent to Chief Superintendent at the Sûreté, which is France's Scotland Yard.

"Come in, *mon vieux*," said Letord, shaking him warmly by the hand. "Why do you so seldom come? It is too long since we met, far too long. Sit down, please. Excuse me one moment." He rang a bell on his desk and immediately a man came in.

"I am engaged," said Letord. "If anybody except Monsieur the President of France wants me, I am not to be disturbed. If Monsieur the President wants me, I have gone to heaven and you do not know when my ghost may be expected to return. That is all, go!"

The man vanished and Hambledon laughed.

"I always admired the way you discipline your subordinates," he said. "If I were one of them I should not dare to sit down for fear there would not be time to get up."

"So they think," said Letord. "Now tell me all about yourself. I suppose you have been in the usual series of troubles, eh? Out of one frying pan into the next fire? My friend, you are made of asbestos. When I sit quiet in the evening and the welcome picture of you rises upon the screen of my mind, I see you surrounded by corpses, always."

"Oh, please not," said Hambledon. "How very unpleasant."

"Not at all. Your sportsmen in England, when they have a shooting, the birds and beasts are all laid out in rows, are they not? Deer on the left, foxes in the middle, hares on the right, and pheasants all along the front, and there, towering above all, the sportsman with his gun, for the photograph, no? Certainly. So it is when I think of you. Magnificent."

Eventually Hambledon managed to steer Letord to the subject of the Arnage murders.

"Tell me all about them," said Letord, "from the beginning. I do not receive these country reports unless we are called in, as you know."

Hambledon did as he was asked and ended: "Power was working with your people on a case in Paris before all this blew up at Arnage. A financier who was murdered, is that right?"

Letord nodded. "Marius Aldebert. But we are not quite sure about it; it might have been suicide. It looked like suicide, but it may have been murder made to look like suicide. I am not pleased about that case. We work hard and use such wits as the good God gave us, and attain no finality. His flat was sealed up and guarded after the body was removed, but it was broken into all the same. I would like to know why. There were both money and valuables there, but they were not taken."

"There was a fingerprint——"

"Certainly there was, but it is not on record. You sent me up another which the poor young Power found; he was right, it is the same. Tell me how and where he found it. . . . I see. These stands of postcards, everyone fingers them, do they not? How many people in that hotel?"

"About eighty. Plus the staff. There are also passing travellers who drop in for a meal."

Letord lifted his hands and dropped them. "You see? It is like that, this case, when one is given anything it is no help. I repeat, I am not happy about that case. Marius Aldebert's brother, Julius Aldebert, he is not happy either, and every little while he comes round here to see me and says he pays his taxes and the taxes pay us but when his brother is murdered we sit and do nothing."

"So he thinks——"

"Oh yes, he thinks it is murder. A psychological reason. 'My brother would never commit suicide, therefore he did not, therefore it is murder. Find me the assassin!' You have met people who argue like that? Yes, yes, the world is full of them. The tiresome thing is that they are so often right. So now he has engaged the Spiders."

"The what?"

"Spiders Anonymous. With a motto: 'We spread webs, we

catch men.' Private enquiry agents. Spider himself—his name is Jean Jaboulet, but everyone calls him Spider—is an extraordinary type. My friend, he thinks he is Vidocq returned to life. He has a little office in a narrow street off the Boulevard des Italiens—you know those little streets? There is a front entrance and a back entrance. The staff and the clients come in at the front entrance; Spider comes in at the back, straight into his private room, and only his head clerk has ever seen him and even he does not always recognize him."

"What? But that's absurd."

"Not so absurd. Spider is a master of disguise, and his head clerk, who only goes in when his bell rings, never knows whether he is going to see a country farmer or a ragpicker or a general of artillery or a detective superintendent of the Sûreté. Not only his clothes change, but his face looks different; his manner, his carriage, his habits, his walk—all vary in accordance with what he is. His head clerk does the office work and a number of bright young men go out on assignments, but Spider likes to deal with the important ones himself. The point is that nobody knows what he, Spider, looks like, so that he is never recognized. Vidocq did the most incredible things and carried them off."

"In the days before electric light was invented," said Hambledon. "Also there were no fingerprints in Vidocq's day."

"And I have not got Spider's. But, my friend, you say to yourself that Letord describes a comic, a figure of fun, but you would be wrong. He gets results, this Spider, amazing results by his methods, sometimes when we police have failed, and he likes the limelight on his successes. He is an exhibitionist who hides himself, a showman who never shows himself. So Aldebert's brother engaged him. It will cost money, for Spiders Anonymous charge, *mon Dieu*, colossal sums. But the Aldeberts have all the money there is."

"How nice, or is it? It is of no use being so rich if one is to be murdered for it. Now, about Rougisson."

Letord laughed. "That poor Rougisson! I can tell you something about him, but this is strictly between ourselves, eh? Not even for the so dutiful police of Orleans and district. Rougisson went away—when?—fifteen days ago, saying to everyone, including his wife, that he was going to North Africa to study bird migration.

No letters need be expected because where his birds lived there were no post offices. My friend, no doubt I have an unkind and suspicious mind, but I did not know that North Africa was so uncivilized and thinly populated as that. So his wife thought also, or perhaps she had other sources of information such as letters not intended for her eyes, or even cheque stubs. His birds, she said, have no feathers except, possibly, in their hats. You see, there is little love lost between Monsieur and Madame Rougisson. Perhaps they have been married a little too long, do you think? Twenty-two years is a long time."

"It is of no use to ask me," said Hambledon. "I have never been married for even six months."

"Nor I. Nor I. I have considered the matter sometimes, but always there has been something more urgent to be done. Well now, Madame, holding these views, did not believe the birds were so far off as North Africa and so she put Spiders Anonymous on his tail. I do not know what success they have had, but if there is anything to find out they will find it."

"That will cost her something, if Spiders Anonymous charge as you say they do."

"My poor friend!" Of course Monsieur would pay. Naturally. That was why I said 'poor Rougisson' just now."

"But now he is dead, she will have to pay it herself out of the estate."

"Out of the insurance money, *mon vieux*. Listen, and forget this as soon as you have heard it. You promise? For this is like those documents they say you British endorse on the outside: 'Most completely top secret. Burn before reading.' Eh? As soon as he had gone away Madame went to an insurance company and insured Monsieur's life for I do not know how much. A very nice sum indeed if one were soon to be left a widow and therefore did not have to pay many large premiums. Eh? You understand. When he is killed, the Orleans police ring up the Paris police, who send a man to her flat to tell her the sad news. The death certificate, he says, will follow to enable Madame to arrange the obsequies of the so distinguished Monsieur Rougisson. What does she say? Alas, alas for the grief. Does she weep? No. She says, 'Two copies, please, I want one for the insurance company.' So two copies are sent and the moment she has them—the same moment, *mon vieux*—she trots off to the insurers and says, 'Look at this. My fifty million francs, please.' "

Hambledon whistled.

"Or some such amount. So the insurance people say: 'Accept, madame, this expression of our most melancholy condolences. We will put this matter through the office and you shall receive our cheque without the slightest delay. Yes, madame, certainly. No, madame, certainly not.' So they bow her out and immediately come running to me. What? Deplorable, yes, but human nature is what it is and insurance companies do not believe in fairies. Nor in fairy stories either. Is this one, do you think?"

"To the best of my belief, no," said Hambledon. "Rougisson was shot at the foot of a ladder at my bedroom window by a man who had just climbed down it. At least, that's not quite literally true—the ladder fell down and so did the man—but it's not a long drop, and when he fell he was being held by the wrists. He would not hurt himself. In fact, he did not; he shot Rougisson and ran away. He—the man in my room—was interested in Power, not Rougisson with or without girl friends."

"You are perfectly certain," said Letord keenly, "that Rougisson was shot by the man in your room and not by a third man possibly stalking him in the garden?"

"Quite sure. I have an eyewitness." Hambledon repeated what Campbell had seen that night and added: "There were only two men there, struggling together, and one of them fired the shot and ran away. The other fell down. That was Rougisson."

"I see. It looks as though the insurance company are going to be unlucky. It does not matter, they have plenty of money. I will remind them of that when I ring them up. Tell me, why did your burglar shoot Rougisson dead instead of tripping him up and running away? Or clumping him on the head with the butt of the gun? Why kill him—why shoot and awaken the neighbourhood? Murders should have a motive, and this one seems inadequate. You say it was dark. It was not a question of silencing one who had seen his face. Was he in a high state of nervous excitement?"

"On the contrary, I thought him unpleasantly calm."

"It does not fit," said Letord gloomily, and Hambledon looked up.

"It is odd you should use that phrase. It is what the Superintendent at Orleans is always saying about these two cases. 'But, Monsieur, it does not fit.'"

"He is a sensible man if he says the same as I. About Monsieur Power, I was sorry about that. I liked him, he had intelligence. Thank you for sending up the cartridge case; that will be more help than the bullet in identifying the gun. That is, if we are vouchsafed the right gun to identify; those that were sent up from Arnage may all be innocent, you know. Our ballistic experts are working on them now; you shall have the results in a few days' time. I hope they are not all—what do the Americans say? Nix? Let us pray. About Rougisson . . ."

Letord's voice tailed off and he sank into meditation, his eyes staring blankly at nothing. Hambledon waited a few minutes and then prompted him gently.

"About Rougisson?"

Letord woke up.

"I am still not satisfied, and if I am not satisfied, believe me, the insurance company will not be either. There is too much of mystery about the death of Rougisson. What do we know? That he was shot, that is all."

"By an unknown man who was in my——"

"I know, I know. You say 'man'; how do you know it was not a woman? He or she only whispered, you tell me."

"She had a stiff beard then," said Hambledon, "and it did not come off in the scrimmage."

"Good, good. A man, then, but you notice that if he had happened to be clean-shaven we should not even have been sure of that. These unknown men! Listen, my friend. Rougisson was often away for considerable periods, and Madame had no taste for solitude. She had friends, men friends. I make no suggestions, but there were men who went to her flat—I will tell you frankly what put me on this line; it was her reception of the news of his death. I told you. 'Two copies, please, of the certificate, one for the insurance company.' Who told her to say that? Does it not sound like a man's advice? And why give that advice if one were not expecting someone to die? A man could go down the Rue de Lappe any night and hire a man with a gun to do a job of work. I do not say that she could so easily, but a man could.

She hears from Spiders Anonymous: 'Your husband is at Arnage.' She insures his life. Then the unknown man goes down and bang! There is the insurance money and possibly a nice new husband in the background waiting till the dust settles. Eh?"

"Nonsense," said Hambledon. "Why should he bring a ladder and climb up to my room? He would be much better sitting in a bush in the garden till Rougisson should return."

"That was done for a blind, to make you think he was a burglar disturbed——"

"I suppose he arranged for Lacroix to see the ladder and send the night porter up to drop your gunman out of my window at exactly the right moment."

Letord waved his hand in the gesture of one driving away flies. "Something went wrong, that is all——"

"Very wrong. As for the advice about the death certificate, she could have got that—as information, not advice—from any friend whose husband had been killed in an accident. 'I had to get a second certificate.' You are building a castle upon a molehill, my dear Letord."

"Tell me why he had to be shot," said Letord obstinately.

"I wish somebody would tell me why Rougisson broke into the mortuary to look at Power's head. To my mind, that is far more mysterious," said Hambledon.

"Yes, that is true. I can see no sense in that, myself, but it is his death with which I am concerned, I and the insurance company."

"Will they pay up?"

"Not all, of course. A substantial instalment to keep her quiet and a string of excuses about the delay in paying the rest. He will be buried at Père Lachaise the day after tomorrow—Thursday—with full rites of Holy Church and carriages full of flowers and mourners, representing learned societies, walking two by two in top hats. Tell me, you who know so many odd things, what demented brain devised the top hat?"

"I have sometimes wondered that myself. By the way, before I go," said Hambledon, pulling out his wallet, "there is one thing, though it may not be of the slightest use. Power had made a note of a telephone number; here it is."

Letord took it. "It is a Paris number," he said, and reached out for his desk telephone. "Get me Telephone Enquiries, please. Thank you. . . . Of course it might be anything; his hairdresser, his—— Is that Telephone Enquiries? Sûreté speaking. I have a Paris telephone number here, be so good as to give me the name and address of the subscriber." He read it out and added: "Yes, immediately, if you will be so good. Thank you. . . . I was going to say his laundry, but it is no matter. As you say, there is no reason to expect it to help us, but we may as well try. 'Allo, yes? Oh, is it? Thank you." He wrote down something on his pad. "A thousand thanks. Au 'voir. Here you are."

The note, in Letord's spiky writing, announced: "Café de Bruges, Rue de l'Arbre Vert, 21, Arrondissement 11."

"Not a fashionable neighbourhood," said Hambledon. "Do you know anything about the Café de Bruges?"

"The name says something to me," said Letord thoughtfully, "but not loud enough for me to hear. I will have it looked up for you and see if there is anything in the records. You would like this at once?"

"No, no," said Hambledon, "I must get back to Arnage now. I shall be in Paris again very soon, no doubt."

"When you come, if we have anything about the Café de Bruges, you shall have it.'

"By the way," said Hambledon, "there was one other rather mysterious object in Power's pocket." He took out the little silver box containing the three beans and showed them to Letord, who shook his head.

"I do not know anything about beans," he said.

Campbell and Forgan, at Arnage-sur-Loire, spent their time driving or strolling about and sometimes walked at night too.

"I begin to suffer," said Campbell gloomily, "from a feeling of frustration. I moon about here making a public exhibition of myself which will be handed down in the annals of Arnage for twenty generations to come, and with what result? Nothing." He threw up his head and howled like a dog. "Wa—hoo—o!"

"For heaven's sake," said Forgan, "not when we're alone. You're letting this become a habit."

"It could, you know."

Forgan looked at him rather anxiously and said: "Let's take the car out and go somewhere where nobody knows us. Let's go to Chartres and look at stained-glass windows and eat *pâtés*. Let's go and watch somebody playing golf, that's always funny. Let's go to Orleans and ask that old imbecile Delamere to show us his bugs. Let's go——"

"Let's go, anyway," agreed Campbell, so they ordered Arthur and the Rolls and drove out and about. Campbell, lulled by the easy motion of the Rolls, went to sleep for an hour and woke up more cheerful.

"I don't know what I'm moaning about," he said. "It's only two days since our last murder; it is positively immoral to expect people to go on bumping each other off for our amusement. It is unreasonable. Isn't it, Forgan?"

"Perhaps Hambledon will have acquired some leading in Paris. Let's go back, he may be home by now."

They turned for Arnage and had almost reached it when the Rolls engine coughed in a ladylike manner, sneezed once, and fell silent. Arthur coasted in to the side of the road and stopped, and Campbell leaned forward.

"What now, Phoebus, what now?"

"Petrol," said the chauffeur shortly, and got out of the car. "That gauge needle's stuck again, it misled me. All right, all right, it's my fault, I should 'ave fixed it."

"You should indeed," said Forgan, rather annoyed. "You'd better go and get some; we'll wait here."

Half an hour later Campbell was sitting in the sun on the bank at the side of the road; Forgan had strolled on. A small boy, staggering a little under the load of a sack on his shoulders, came along the road, eyed the Rolls, looked at Campbell, and slowed down. Then he swung the sack off his shoulders and stopped.

"*Bo'jour*, m'sieu'. "

"*Bonjour*," said Campbell, and grinned at him.

"Will your car not go?"

"No, not just at present. We have run out of petrol."

"Oh. I thought perhaps it was the water was not good for her."

"The water?" said Campbell, puzzled. "What water?"

"But, the Flood, m'sieu'."

"The flood?"

"But, in the Bible, m'sieu', we are told about it, and in the village they say yours is an automobile of the most magnificent but it was made before the Flood."

"I see. I think she has recovered from that now; it is a long time ago, you know."

The boy nodded. "Before I was born."

"That's right. We have had her done up since then. What have you got in your sack?"

"Greenstuff. For my rabbit."

"Rabbit? I thought all the rabbits round here had died of myxomatosis."

"Not my rabbit. She is a—a—chilincha."

"Chinchilla?"

"That is it, m'sieu'. Beautiful grey."

"You were lucky that she didn't catch it."

"She wasn't born then. Now she's the only rabbit anywhere round here except M'sieu' Barbeau's."

Campbell lit a cigarette.

"Who is Monsieur Barbeau?"

"A farmer. He lives over there. He gave me mine."

"That was nice of him, wasn't it?"

The boy smiled. "Her mother had such a lot and my rabbit wasn't getting enough and she was going to die, so he gave her to me and she didn't die."

"Very good indeed. You must have taken a lot of trouble."

"Yes. Then my father brought home some cattle oil-cake. Cattle cake is good for rabbits."

"I must remember that."

"She's a lovely rabbit now—but, enormous." The boy spanned with his arms a space which would have done credit to an outsize tom cat. "M'sieu' Barbeau wants her back now, but I won't let him."

"I should think not, indeed. He was going to let her die."

"Yes. She's my rabbit and I won't let her go. Are you the poor gentleman who isn't right in the head?"

"I am, yes. Why?"

"I think you seem all right to me."

"I get attacks," said Campbell, thinking that the boy would probably talk when he got home.

"Like my *gran'mère*. She gets them in her legs, sometimes one and sometimes both. They swell up. Does your head swell up?"

"Not much, now. I have a kind doctor who is making me better; here he comes along the road."

The boy picked up his sack and rolled it on to his shoulder.

"I must go now. Au 'voir, m'sieu'."

"What is your name?"

"Armand Salle, m'sieu'."

"Au 'voir, Armand. And long life to your rabbit."

"Thank you, m'sieu'."

HAMBLEDON returned from Paris with no news except a story about an extraordinary character called Spider, but as no one knew what he looked like, where he was, or what he was doing, if anything, it did not seem as though it would be of much help.

Next morning Vidal tapped at Hambledon's bedroom door while he was shaving, and came in with a piece of news.

"The gun has been identified, monsieur. The one which was used to shoot Monsieur Power."

"But that is magnificent! Sit down and have a cigarette. Have a—— I haven't much to offer unless you'd like a tooth-glassful of warm water with a dash of Dettol? I've never been one of those people who keep whisky on the washstand—— Whose gun was it?"

"It belongs to an elderly farmer named Barbeau, Jules Barbeau. His farm is that one just outside the village astride the road to Paris, you know? Yes. My Superintendent came out from Orleans early this morning to question him. We were not satisfied, so we took him in to Orleans and now the whole family are in there too, all baying like bloodhounds and contradicting each other."

"I don't envy your Superintendent," said Hambledon. "I think I must have seen Barbeau, a tall old man with stick-out eyebrows and a mouth like a rattrap? Yes. What a to-do there will be in the village."

There was, indeed, for the village knew something which Hambledon did not.

Barbeau's sons had clubbed together to give him the rifle on his sixtieth birthday some ten years earlier, for the old man had been an extremely good shot in those days. One needs to be, to shoot rabbits with a .22 rifle. It was a folding gun; that is, it was hinged just behind the lock so that the stock could fold back along the barrel, and it also had a silencer on it; Barbeau used to go out in the evenings when the rabbits were feeding, make his way through a strip of woodland to a meadow which was their favourite stamping ground, and pick them off at his leisure. If one rabbit rolls over dead, the others take no notice if they see no one and hear no sound.

With the passage of years Barbeau's sight became gradually impaired and there were one or two regrettable incidents, fortunately of a minor character. His family—he had two sons, two daughters-in-law, and an orphaned but useful niece—regarded with unmitigated terror the prospect of having to try to persuade Barbeau not to go out shooting any more. Barbeau was the type of man politely called a patriarch or, in moments of exasperation, an iron-jawed old tyrant. However, the family was spared this ordeal by the advance of science. Myxomatosis reduces not only rabbits but also the number of people potting at them. Barbeau was thus reduced, everyone who had to do with him sighed with relief, and the gun was hung upon two nails in the wall of the back kitchen, to be taken down, cleaned, and replaced every Sunday after Mass.

The moment that it became known that the gun which had been used to shoot Power was that belonging to Barbeau, an awed hush spread round Arnage-sur-Loire, and the village people looked at each other, saying "Ah" in muted tones. Constable Maroche did not ask why, because he knew already. Barbeau had had one of his famous quarrels with Alan Power; all Barbeau's quarrels were of an epic character, but this one was outstanding. True, he had had provocation.

About ten years earlier Barbeau had been persuaded into buying an incubator, oil-lamp-heated. He spent a couple of long evenings poring over the directions for use and rejected with contumely his younger son's offer to show him how to work it. He then put eighty-seven eggs into it, lit the lamp, and waited for the appointed time.

One egg hatched out a handsome Rhode Island Red chick.

Barbeau said that somebody had let the cold air in out of idle curiosity, probably feminine, and his family knew better than to argue. They kept out of his way while he cleared out the mis-fires and tucked up the surviving chick in a bird cage near the kitchen range. It grew, flourished, and became exceedingly friendly, especially with Barbeau, who called it Alphonse.

Barbeau, ordaining that no one but himself should in future so much as approach the incubator, drew a chalk circle round the apparatus on the barn floor after the method usually employed by magicians for repelling evil spirits, dared his family to put one foot across the line, and tried again with seventy-seven eggs this time.

On the third night the lamp smoked, flared up, destroyed the incubator, and burned the barn to the ground. On this occasion both daughters-in-law went home to their mothers for a few days and the intrepid niece carried on alone. She was nearly stone-deaf and was therefore spared much.

Alphonse grew daily in grace and beauty, developing also a surprising degree of intelligence, as even fowls do if made into pets, talked to and played with every day. He even learned a few simple tricks. Barbeau took pride in saying that he owned the most expensive cock in the whole world, for he had cost 257,482 francs, the value of the incubator, the barn, the paraffin oil ex-pended, and a hundred and sixty-four eggs. Years passed by and Alphonse became a familiar figure, for wherever Barbeau went Alphone pattered after. Except, of course, to Mass. The old man would come out of his house and snap his fingers and Alphonse, abandoning all else, would utter chawking noises and rush after him, until one day when Alan Power came down the road from Paris in his red sports car.

Old Barbeau crossed the road from his farm gate before the red car passed; Alphonse, who was beginning to feel his years, was slow in following him. There was a terrified squawk and a flurry of feathers. . . .

Power stopped the car and backed to the farm gate to apologize and offer to pay, since, although it was in no sense his fault, he had seen and heard about Alphonse, and the thing was a tragedy.

Barbeau was quite beyond apologies and, when offered money, demanded 257,482 francs, which was manifestly absurd, and Power said so. The old man, nursing his dead fowl, was beside himself with fury. He yelled, stamped, and swore, and his terrified family peered round corners and from behind curtains. Power spoke to the eldest son, who had put his head timidly out of the door.

"I'm terribly sorry," he said, "but I think your father's going mad."

"*Mais oui*," said the eldest son, and disappeared from sight. Power tried again.

"Monsieur Barbeau, I am completely desolated. I regret, from the bottom of my heart, this unhappy accident. I could not avoid——"

Barbeau uttered a most savage roar and rushed into the house. One of the ground-floor windows was flung open and a daughter-in-law thrust her head out.

"Fly, monsieur, fly instantly! He has gone for his gun!"

Power ran to his car, leapt into the driving seat, and drove hastily away. He glanced into the driving mirror and saw Barbeau run out of the house with his gun in his hand. Power put his foot hard down as the old man fired. Power took a corner on two wheels and did not stop until he was in the yard of the Hotel de la Poste.

"You know," said Power, telling his story in the bar to a group which included Farelli and the hotel manager, "that old man's dangerous. Something ought to be done about it."

So the villagers looked out of the corners of their eyes and whispered together.

The most important point at issue was, of course, where Barbeau was at eleven o'clock on the morning of the murder, for the evidence of both Dr. Farelli and the lorry driver established that the red MG went over the brink within a minute or so, one way or the other, of 11 A.M. Barbeau said he was at home in his own house and defied the police to prove otherwise. The police said that it was not for them to prove otherwise, it was for Barbeau to prove his statement. Barbeau's assembled family all began at once to offer corroborative evidence in loud or shrill voices, from which it appeared that they had all been in the kitchen together at eleven that morning.

"All together, eh?" said the Superintendent, who had himself been brought up on a farm. "At eleven in the morning? That is not dinnertime. When is the work done on your farm?"

The simultaneous clamour began again, the Superintendent roared them into silence, and quite suddenly old Barbeau lost his temper. He cursed the police for arresting him, his family for chattering like a pack of starlings, Power for existing at all, and the world in general for incommoding Barbeau.

"You babbling, brainless nitwits," he bawled at his family, "telling a tale so stupid that even a policeman does not believe it! Of course they were not in the house at that time; I was, and if I had seen any of them loitering about instead of working I should have put my stick round their legs! As for Power, I did not shoot him, I wish I had. He deserved it, he killed Alphonse. I wish I did know who shot him, I should like to thank him. I did have a shot at him once, but unfortunately I missed. As for you who call yourselves police and go about dressed up in uniforms, looking silly and arresting the wrong people, why can't you do a job of work and stop these motorists rushing about killing things? I don't know what the world's coming to, I don't really. If you want to know who killed that Power, go and find out. Why arrest me?"

"Because it was done with your gun," said the Superintendent slowly and distinctly.

"Nonsense. It could not have been."

"It was."

"You lie. You are pinning it on me because you can't think of anyone else to charge. You——"

"Listen, Barbeau, and try to take this in. We have not only the bullet but also the empty cartridge case, and both carry marks which show they were fired from your gun and no other."

"I don't believe it. Marks! Do you suggest that my gun was dirty?"

"When did you clean it last?"

"What business is that of yours?"

"You had better answer my questions, Barbeau, you are in a very serious position."

"You put me there and you can get me out again. I won't answer your stupid questions. My gun is always clean."

"Then you clean it regularly?"

Barbeau appeared not to hear, and the Superintendent transferred his question to the quivering row of family witnesses.

"Does he?"

They all nodded their heads silently.

"When does he usually clean it? When? Answer me or I'll put the whole lot of you in the cells!"

The eldest daughter-in-law spoke up. "Every Sunday after Mass," and Barbeau whirled round on her.

"How dared you answer when I forbade you?"

"But if we are all in prison, who will feed the stock?"

Barbeau turned away his head; apparently even he could see the sense of that.

"Barbeau," said the Superintendent, "did you clean your gun last Sunday?"

"Yes."

"And was the barrel fouled? Had it been used?"

Barbeau thought this over for some time and eventually said: "No."

The eldest son looked up with a startled expression, and the Superintendent, who was intently watching the whole family, noticed it. He raised his voice so that even the deaf niece, hand cupped behind ear, heard it.

"Barbeau! Think again. When you cleaned your gun last Sunday, was the barrel fouled? Speak the truth!"

"No, it wasn't. I told you, it was——"

His niece broke in, in the loud, flat voice of the very deaf.

"You've forgotten, Uncle! You said it was dirty, Uncle! Then you beat Étienne because you said he had——"

"Silence!" bellowed Barbeau, and added an ugly epithet. "You must not take any notice of what she says," he went on to the Superintendent. "She's half-witted, always was. I only keep her out of charity."

The Superintendent looked at the niece's draggled grey hair, bent figure, and toil-worn hands and said, "Charity," under his breath. However, the niece was no concern of his.

"So the gun was——" he began, but Barbeau cut in.

"Now I come to think back, I am none so sure I did clean it last Sunday. I was late coming home from Mass and when I got in, dinner was ready, so I sat down to it right away." He looked round at his palpitating family on the bench behind him. "That's right, isn't it?"

"That is right," they chorused. "You were in late."

"Didn't clean the gun at all last Sunday," concluded Barbeau triumphantly. "So, as it was clean when you took it away, it had not been used that week. See? It was not my gun as shot Power, see? You and your silly marks!" Barbeau laughed with what sounded like genuine amusement and probably was.

The police enquiry went on, the Superintendent introducing such awkward topics as ammunition possessed by Barbeau, finger-prints, alibis, and so forth. Practically every member of the family seemed to have run into the farmhouse upon some pretext or another round about eleven o'clock. Not together, no. For different reasons, naturally. Why had Barbeau chastised his son? For neglecting to feed the pigs, of course. And so on, interminably.

Eventually the Superintendent gave it up for the present; had the old man removed, with furious protests, to the cells and the rest of the family dismissed. When the room was at last empty and quiet, the Superintendent leaned back in his chair with a heavy sigh, wiped his forehead with his handkerchief, and spoke partly to himself and partly to one of his inspectors who was hovering sympathetically.

"When this case was first proved to be murder," said the Superintendent in a low angry growl, "I implored Heaven not to make it another Dominici case, and now look at it. Curse these infernal Englishmen who come to France to get themselves murdered! The trouble they give! Two solid hours and we are no further."

The Barbeau family, without their distinguished head, re-turned to Arnage-sur-Loire and immediately held an indignation meeting in the middle of the village street. Except, of course, for the deaf niece, who had only the vaguest idea of what had been happening at Orleans.

"I go home," she said loudly. "I go to cook the dinner. Some-body must, *hein?* When he comes home he will be angry again." She turned on her heel and padded off along the road alone, while the villagers gathered round to hear the news, which in half an hour's time was being discussed and argued about in every house in the place. Hambledon heard it in the tobacconist's shop from his friend the proprietress, who had extracted every detail from the elder son's wife when she came in to buy tobacco for her husband.

"It is very serious," said the proprietress. "Very serious indeed, and one cannot wonder if they are upset. No one can wish the head of one's household to be taken up for murder, monsieur, whatever he may be like."

"No, indeed not. Though I understand that Barbeau in the home was sometimes a trifle exacting, though one cannot of course believe all one hears."

"Whatever Monsieur has heard is probably less than the truth. A Turk, that Barbeau, a veritable Turk. Picture to yourself, monsieur, that he would take his stick to those others as though they were disobedient children, full grown as they are? Yes, men and women alike, and that Étienne, he must be forty-five, the eldest son."

"What? Do you really mean he used to strike his sons' wives?"

She nodded portentously. "If I had been one of them and he had but lifted his stick to me, he would have got the contents of the nearest pot in his face, chance if it was boiling!"

"And you would have been fully justified, madame."

"So I think. But that will not stop them from misleading the police in all ways possible, monsieur, and that is right too. One must stand by one's own."

CHAPTER 10 *Room Telephone*

WHEN HAMBLEDON finally disengaged himself from the tobacconist's shop, the first person he met was Police Constable Maroche wearing a dissatisfied expression which brightened when he saw Hambledon.

"Good day, monsieur." Maroche came up close and dropped his voice to a discreet murmur. "Detective Sergeant Vidal has told me in the strictest confidence, which must be preserved at all costs, that Monsieur is our colleague, in a sense."

"It is very important," said Hambledon urgently, "that no one should even guess, for my usefulness is lost if it is known."

"Yes, monsieur. For me, I am glad, for in a case involving an Englishman, another Englishman should be a help."

"Thank you, Maroche, I will do all I can, believe me. But, as regards Monsieur Power, I hear that you have arrested the farmer Barbeau."

Maroche's dissatisfied expression returned.

"The Orleans police arrested him, monsieur, not I. I would not have done so unless under the most stringent orders because, monsieur, Barbeau did not do it."

"This is most interesting. Please go on."

"I have been thinking," said Maroche heavily. "There is a case against him, yes. It was his gun, he had shot at Monsieur Power before, he had uttered threats, he had had provocation—Monsieur has heard about Alphonse?—and I very much doubt if he has an alibi. And Vidal found ammunition when he searched the farm. Yes, there is a case. But it is wrong. Barbeau, monsieur, was a good shot once, but now he is so blind he could not hit a barn unless, as they say, he was inside it with the door shut. I have known Barbeau for twenty years, and sometimes he forgets I am a policeman and talks to me as though I were a Christian—

93

Monsieur knows what I mean. A year ago Barbeau told me that if he sighted along his rifle he saw two back sights and, as it were, a tuft of wool where the front sight should be, and not always that. Also, whoever fired the shot smoked cigarettes—we found the butts—Barbeau smokes a pipe. Again, he who fired the shot knew Monsieur Power was coming and lay in wait, yes? How was Barbeau to know if Monsieur Power was going on this road or that, or at what time? Find who knew that, monsieur, and we shall be nearer the mark. Finally, monsieur—forgive me, I even remind myself of the curé with his sermons—finally, Barbeau would not do it if he could. He flies into furies of the most daunting, yes, and hits out at anyone then, but it is flare-up and pass. Alphonse was killed a month ago—yes, more than that. Monsieur Power was absent from here three weeks and it was before that. Barbeau would never lie in wait, in cold blood, three weeks later, to kill a man for a red cock. Never." Maroche took his kepi off to rub his head and smiled suddenly. "All this thinking, eh? Monsieur is very patient——"

"Not at all. Everything you have said is of the utmost interest. Can it be that the Orleans police do not know what you know?"

"Monsieur, I am a wooden-headed country constable who will never be a sergeant though my hair is now grey——"

"Maroche, I will repeat what your Superintendent in Orleans said to me about you. He said, 'Maroche looks slow but he is nobody's fool and he knows his village as I know my own family.'"

"I thank Monsieur. He said that, did he? I should have spoken in any case, but now I shall do it in better heart. But imagine it, monsieur. For a village constable to approach these clever superintendents and inspectors who have a good case in a murder, and say, 'You have there the wrong man,' monsieur, it is to part the tiger from his prey! *Formidable!*"

Hambledon laughed, encouraged him, and went on his way. Had he known the Superintendent's views about "another Dominici case," he would have been more encouraging still.

He returned to the hotel and encountered Forgan.

"I should like a word with you two if it can be managed."

"Come up to our room, Campbell is there already. Choose your moment to go in unobserved. I'll follow in a few minutes."

Hambledon chose a time when there was no one in the corridor

and went quickly along to the door of their private sitting-room;
even as he opened the door he heard the sound of a tin whistle
played softly.

> Sur le pont d'Avignon
> L'on y passe, l'on y danse,
> Sur le pont d'Avignon
> L'on y danse tous en rond.

The tune broke off as he entered, and Campbell looked up with
a smile.

"I don't know," he said, "why a tendency to penny-whistling
should be regarded as a little peculiar. I think it's rather a nice
noise, myself, though for some reason I don't understand I can't
play 'The Campbells Are Coming' on it. Either I am not expert
enough or the right notes aren't here."

"That reminds me," said Hambledon. "Do you remember
dancing in the hall because a lady mentioned oranges on the
night Rougisson died? Yes, well, an Englishman who was here
then—he's gone now—said your dance reminded him of the
Highland Fling."

"Tiresomely percipient Sassenach."

"Yes, aren't we all?"

"No," said Campbell firmly. "But it is, perhaps, just as well
I can't play 'The Campbells Are Coming.' Somebody might
recognize it even in my rendering, unlikely as it may appear. Here's
Forgan."

"You've heard the news?" said Hambledon. "That Barbeau has
been arrested for Power's murder?"

"Yes, we've heard that," said Forgan. "Motive: because Power
killed his pet cock. Proof: because it was his gun what did it. I
don't know that it would convince me."

"It doesn't convince Maroche," said Hembledon, and repeated
the policeman's argument.

"As for who knew that Power was taking the Orleans road,"
said Campbell, "the answer is, anyone who happened to be in
the lounge when he said so. We were, and quite a number of other
hotel guests also. Power went up to the desk and told the clerk
that he—Power—would not be in to lunch that day as he was
going to lunch in Orleans."

"About ten minutes or so later, our Manager Lacroix came dashing in quite red in the face. He went into the office and swung the door shut so roughly that it merely swung open again. Quite pettish, he was," said Forgan.

"His voice, therefore, treacled out through the open door and was audible in the lounge when he rang up the local *garagiste*. Jacques was to come instantly, but instantly Lacroix speaking, the manager of the Hotel de la Poste. There were two flat tyres on his Citroën, yes, two. One back and the spare. He, Lacroix, had to drive out instantly upon an urgent errand and Jacques was to come immediately, at the run, remove the two wheels and repair the punctures without any delay at all. Urgent, urgent. Leave everything and come. The manager speaking. Well—have you met Jacques, Hambledon?"

Tommy shook his head. "I've had no occasion to, having no car here."

"We have, of course, apropos of the Rolls. He's one of those men who 'wun't be druv,' as they say of Sussex folk. He's quite a good chap and a fair mechanic, but he's singlehanded, and if he once let himself be stampeded he'd be lost. However, he came up quite soon, put the Citroën up on the jack, took off the afflicted back wheel and the spare, and went away with them, rolling one with each hand. Fascinating. It reminded me of the days when porters used to roll two milk churns at once, one in each hand, down long platforms with clanking noises. Remember?"

"When milk churns were abolished," said Hambledon, "an art was lost in England. Go on."

"Lacroix rushed out and squeaked at him, but Jacques merely looked scornfully," said Forgan, "and rolled away. Peace supervened until about half an hour later Power came out to the lockups and wanted to get his MG out. Well, the Citroën was well up against his doors; you might have got a specially thin bicycle out, but no more. So Power blew up. He was not a very patient person. He rushed round hunting for Lacroix, but he was nowhere to be found."

"In our opinion," said Campbell, "Lacroix had gone to ground under his bed. Or in his wardrobe. Anyway, he didn't show up. Power more or less strode restlessly about for another half hour or so and then went down to the garage to encourage Jacques.

When he got there, the two Citroën wheels were propped up against the garage wall, still flat, and Jacques was nowhere to be seen. When he came back from attending to a tap which wouldn't stop running at the Widow Lassalle's, Power asked if Jacques couldn't do something about shifting Lacroix's barrow from the MG's doorstep? So Jacques, who liked him, started wrenching the cover off one of the Cit's tyres and Power came back to the hotel. He told us all this himself, and as there didn't seem to be anything we could do about it, we went out for a walk."

"Jacques seemed to have taken some time even then," said Forgan, "as it must have been three quarters of an hour later when we saw Power come along the Orleans road and go over the edge."

"So somebody had the best part of two hours altogether," said Hambledon, "to leave the hotel, get a gun—Barbeau's gun—proceed from the farm to the place of ambush——"

"It's no distance," said Campbell.

"No, it isn't. He arrived at the spot and had time to smoke several Gauloises Bleues before Power came along."

"It occurred to us," said Forgan, "to wonder what, exactly, was the matter with Lacroix's tyres, so we took an opportunity this morning to chatter to Jaques about the embarrassing effects of having two flat tyres at the same time. As we expected, he capped our imaginative efforts with a factual account of Lacroix's troubles. There was nothing wrong with the tyres, nothing. That was why he was so long over them, hunting for a puncture that wasn't there. Somebody had played a joke upon that Lacroix and let the air out via the valves. An old joke, to annoy one who was not, perhaps, popular. That Lacroix, a strange type. The messieurs might perhaps have noticed him?"

"We admitted that we had," said Campbell. "Jacques laughed nastily and started whanging into a large piece of iron with a hammer, so we came away."

"I suppose it's not possible," said Hambledon slowly, "to find anyone who noticed Lacroix's car being backed up against Power's lock-up door?"

"I'm afraid not," said Forgan. "There's no attendant on duty there and people just run cars in and leave them anywhere and at all angles. You know what the French are about parking. It's the commonest sight to see people here manhandling cars about to get their own out; we've had to do it ourselves. No one would notice anyone moving the Citroën; besides, why should they? Hotel guests don't know who other cars belong to."

"No. I've been thinking——" said Hambledon absently.

"Admirable," said Campbell deferentially.

"—about Rougisson," continued Tommy. "He broke into the mortuary, as you know, and was seen examining poor Power's head. And I could bear to know what impelled him to do that. However, he was interested in Power. Now, the man who got into my room the night after the Power enquiry said that he was searching it because it was Power's room. I assume he thought Power might have left something behind. Sorry, more blinding glimpses of the obvious, but that's the way my mind works. The man in my room had a stiff bristling beard and so had Rougisson. It occurred to me to wonder if it was Rougisson in my room, not a stranger; Rougisson who was dropped out of my window by the nightporter. Rougisson was shot dead, why? Because he had brought out the truth about Power's death and might find out some more? Letord, at the Sûreté, brought that out. Why, he said, did your escaping burglar shoot and wake the neighbourhood? Why not just give the other fellow a push and run for it? You said, Campbell, that you couldn't tell which man shot which——"

"That's right. Two dim black objects against a slightly lighter background. If I hadn't been out in the dark for some time I should not have seen anything at all."

"You are suggesting," said Forgan, "that the two murders are connected. If so, the same man——"

"Probably shot them both," said Hambledon. "Though it's only fair to say that the Sûreté have a totally different theory about Rougisson's death. I'm sorry I can't tell you about it because it's really quite funny, but it has nothing whatever to do with Power and personally I don't believe it."

"One moment while I arrange my thoughts," said Campbell. "If it was Rougisson in your room and he was shot intentionally, the man who did it must have known Rougisson was going to be in your room then and come out by the window. I mean, he couldn't have recognized him, it was much too dark."

"Take no notice of him, Hambledon," said Forgan. "He likes

to make things difficult. His grandfather was a wire-puzzle designer, did he tell you?"

"I never met his grandfather," said Hambledon. "But, since we don't know who the man with the gun was, it's useless to speculate on how he knew. What worries me is that we may all be labouring earnestly in entirely the wrong direction. We came out here to hunt out a conspiracy and all we do is to sit round talking about murders. Though I see no alternative at the moment."

"Let's hope we get a fresh break soon," said Forgan.

As for Campbell, he picked up his tin whistle and played very softly the air of "Who killed Cock Robin?"

Forgan and Campbell went in to Orleans and strolled about, getting a general idea of the geography of the town and looking into shopwindows. Campbell's enthralled attention was caught by a gentleman's bathing costume of the eighteen-eighties in the window of a secondhand-clothes shop. Heaven knows who the original owner was or from what ancestral trunk in what cobwebbed attic it had been disinterred, but there it was as good as new and not even moth-eaten. It was a sort of combination garment all in once piece, with sleeves to the elbow and legs below the knees; it was buttoned at both shoulders to enable the wearer to wriggle into it from the top, and since it was made of a woven woollen material it fitted the wearer like a skin. Moreover, it was striped with horizontal bars of black and white, each two inches wide. Campbell dived into the shop to buy it, and the woman behind the counter was, naturally, amused.

"Monsieur desires the bathing costume? But, certainly, monsieur. The material is of the most superlative; let Monsieur feel for himself. And new! One can tell, it has never felt sea water."

"Beautiful," said Campbell. "So soft. So firm. So modest."

The woman laughed. "As for the style, one must admit it to be not of *le dernier cri*, as Monsieur sees. But of surpassing value."

"Madame, when I appear in this at Le Touquet, I shall be the cynosure of all eyes."

"I am assured of it! Monsieur will be the subject of envy and admiration from all who see him. Envy from the gentlemen, monsieur, and admiration from the ladies. Let me wrap it up for Monsieur."

"What," said Forgan when he saw it unwrapped, "what the hell do you want that bit of fancy dress for?"

"To go out in at night. Warm but not cumbersome, close-fitting, seemly and not readily disarranged."

"But you'll stick out of the landscape like——"

"Oh no, I shan't. I can stand back in a hedge looking like a gate or sit on a window sill looking like a venetian blind or lie in a corner of the garden looking like a hen coop. In that case, of course, I should also cluck softly. Excellent camouflage. Think of zebras, Forgan, think of zebras. In cases of emergency I can double myself up into a ball and roll away down the nearest slope looking like a wagon wheel, and if anyone really sees me plainly in a good light, how pleasantly idiotic I shall appear. It's the goods, Forgan."

When they returned to Arnage they encountered Hambledon.

"Vidal has just told me something," said Tommy. "Shall we stroll in the garden and admire the beautiful flowers? I should think it would be a natural thing to do. Yes, well, Vidal says that two new guests arrived here just after lunch and that one of them is a crook he used to know quite well some years back. I gather the crook had reason to be sorry he ever met Vidal, and in point of fact Vidal says the man has behaving himself ever since. Vidal thought he was in Algiers until he and a friend turned up here. Vidal doesn't know the friend but thought it better to keep out of sight of both of them. He pointed them out to me; there they are, sitting at the end table on the terrace. The older one is Vidal's previous acquaintance; incidentally he's got the room next to mine, number 30, I saw him go in there."

"They might, I suppose," said Forgan, "merely be here on an innocent holiday. 'When the enterprising burglar's not aburgling——' "

"Yes, of course," said Hambledon. "One just wonders."

"We will be on the alert," said Campbell.

After dinner Forgan and Campbell sat in the lounge playing old maid quietly together. The hotel wireless was playing softly and the manager was incompletely to be seen through the half-open office door working at papers on his desk. The two crooks came into the lounge, and the desk clerk looked up to wish them good evening.

"I hope you will enjoy your stay here," he said politely, and the elder crook thanked him.

"We are just going for a stroll round the village before it gets dark," he said. "We have never been here before."

"A charming place, Arnage," said the clerk loyally. "The church is well worth a visit."

"Thank you," said the visitor, and strolled out of the door with his friend close at his heels.

Campbell stood up suddenly, abandoning the card game, and said abruptly: "I want a piece of string."

Forgan, in a professionally soothing voice, said: "Certainly, why not? There is plenty in our room; shall we go up?"

"Yes," said Campbell, edging to be off, "but it must be a piece without knots in it."

Forgan stacked up the cards, put them in his pocket, and stood up. "We have a new ball, if you remember," he said, and steered his patient towards the stairs. Campbell varied the journey by jumping up the stairs one at a time, with both feet together; at the top they turned left and disappeared from sight.

"Very sad," said a lady in the lounge, addressing Hambledon. "Such a handsome man, too."

"Yes indeed," said Tommy solemnly.

"Forgan," said Campbell as soon as the door of their room shut behind them, "I am going through that fellow's room. They will be out for half an hour at least and I have my master key." For Campbell had taken an impression from the housemaid's while she was very kindly showing him that there really was not an ichthyosaurus under the bed.

"I hope it works," said Forgan.

"Of course it does; it works our lock all right. What, when I've been making oscillating engines for years, do you think I can't make a key?"

"With a pad saw and a nail file," began Forgan, but Campbell was gone. Forgan hesitated a moment, but there was nothing to be gained by staying in their room, whose windows did not command the entrance to the hotel, so that he could not even watch for the men's return. He went back to the lounge thinking that Hambledon might still be there, but the lady who had pitied

Campbell had begun to tell him about her husband's aunt who also had suffered mentally, and Tommy had fled.

Forgan picked up a paper and sat down to read it. The wireless provided soft background music from *L'Arlésienne*; the manager's office door had swung a little wider open and provided a view of the shining golden head bent over the problem of fitting a cigarette into a holder ten inches long; the desk clerk had nothing to do while Georges, the bartender, was increasingly busy, and the minute hand of the lounge clock crawled slowly on. There was another quarter of an hour before the men were due back, and Campbell was a quick——

The lounge door swung open and the two men came in. One of them glanced up at the clock as, without pausing, they crossed the lounge and went quickly up the stairs.

Forgan was on thorns, but there seemed to be nothing he could do to warn Campbell; if the men had gone to the bar he could have engaged them in conversation, but he could hardly run after two total strangers, crying "Hi!" In public, too, even the manager might think it odd. No, the manager's door was now shut. In any case, it was too late.

Campbell, in Room 30, heard voices at the door and a key rattled in the lock. He closed the lid of the suitcase he had just opened and, without a moment's hesitation, dived under the bed and rolled well into the middle; fortunately the bed was wide.

The door opened, two men came in together, and Campbell heard them lock the door.

"This watch," said one of them angrily, "can go back to the shop. It's lost ten minutes since this morning."

"Lucky I looked at mine," said the other.

"It was, even if it did only cost two thousand francs. I don't know what would have been said if we hadn't been here on time to get our orders."

"You didn't do your watch no good dropping it in the hand basin yesterday. I expect the water has got in it."

"What do you make the time now?"

"Twenty-eight minutes past eight."

"Two minutes," said the other. "I'll set my watch, not that that'll do much good." One man crossed to the window while the other sat down on the edge of the bed and lit a cigarette. Campbell could see their feet and no more; both wore shoes with thick crepe soles, but one pair was brown and the other black. Black was sitting on the bed while Brown was by the window. A long minute passed in silence, and another.

Suddenly the telephone bell rang, and Black, on the bed, started nervously, for Campbell felt the mattress quiver. Brown crossed quickly from the window, picked up the receiver, and said: "Room 30." He then listened in silence, only saying "Yes" at intervals. Finally he said "Thank you" and replaced the receiver.

"Well?" said Black eagerly. "What did he say?"

"It's on tonight," said Brown. "We go to Dupont's place and pick him up, bind him, and put a sack over his head so's he can't see where he's going. Then we take him to St. Antoine's. I stay there with him three days and then let him loose and get away myself. You bring the car straight back here and go to bed. Tomorrow you clock out and go back to Paris. Pay the bill here and tell the clerk I've gone off with some friends."

"What car——"

"We take the car in lock-up number three, the Rolls——"

"What, that hearse?"

"Hearse nothing, it's dead quiet and big enough to hold him comfortably in the back, on the floor. We start from here at half-past twenty-three hours——oh yes, and he said the car key's in an envelope in the bedside cupboard." Brown crossed the room with long strides, but Black leaned over and opened the cupboard door. "Yes, there it is. Give it to me. The garage door will be unlocked."

"What do we say to the night porter?"

"We go out from here shortly, about twenty-one hours, and tell the porter we're going to meet some friends and may be back late. Those are the friends I'm supposed to have gone off with when you come back alone. You can be a bit unsteady, not rolling drunk but having had a nice evening."

Black got up from the bed. "I'd better go up to my own room now, then. I'll put a coat on and get some money——"

"And your gun. I'm taking mine," said Brown, "naturally. May come in useful. You never know." He laughed.

Black went out and Brown spent the intervening time collecting what he would need for the night's enterprise. He seemed to have come prepared, for he opened the lid of the suitcase which Campbell had been about to inspect and took from it a length of thin rope and a large white bag which, if Campbell had been a housewife instead of an engineer, he would instantly have recognized as a pillow case. Brown put these on the floor while he rummaged further in the suitcase. Campbell merely surmised that Brown was getting out a gun of some kind and probably a clasp knife. The suitcase was shut; Brown picked up the rope and the pillow case, threw them on the bed, and put on a light raincoat which was hanging on the back of the door. More putting things in pockets and, in general, the exercise of forethought until there came a knock at the door. Brown unlocked and opened it.

"Well?" said Black's voice. "All ready?"

"All ready," answered Brown. "Let's go."

The door closed and was locked, but Campbell stayed where he was for some time before he rolled out from under the bed and stood up. He wasted no time on completing his unfinished search; what he had heard was far more informative than anything he was likely to find. He let himself out of the room, unseen by any, and went to find Forgan.

FORGAN was standing at the head of the stairs examining under a convenient light a bus timetable of the Orleans district. Not that he was interested in the Orleans omnibus services, having a car of his own, but as an excuse for standing still in any odd place and becoming deeply rapt there is nothing to compare with a bus timetable. From where he stood he could see up and down the stairs and along the diverging corridors which led towards Hambledon's room and their own. When Campbell, unruffled and undamaged, turned the corner and came into sight, Forgan drew a long breath of relief.

Campbell came up to him. "I've got a—a nice piece of string," he said in a low tone.

"Strong enough to hang somebody?"

"Come along."

They went to their room, where Campbell poured out his story. "Where's Hambledon, do you know?" he added.

"I don't," said Forgan. "When I went back to the lounge he'd gone out. We'd better go and look for him."

"There's not too much time," said Campbell, "the balloon goes up at half-past eleven. Two hours' time."

"If we can't find him, do we inform the police? By 'the police' I mean Vidal."

Campbell hesitated. "Vidal—and is he here tonight?—is only on these two murders. I doubt if he knows anything about the big job we're on. I don't know for certain that this kidnapping business is anything to do with our job, either, but it smells like it."

Forgan agreed. "It does, to me. Of course we could balk this kidnapping stunt tonight quite easily by turning up at the moment when they're starting up the Rolls. If we say 'Desist!' what do they do?"

"Let us go and look for Hambledon."

But Hambledon was nowhere to be seen. In point of fact he had encountered Police Constable Maroche in the act of going off duty and was sitting in Maroche's little parlour drinking coffee and hearing stories about Arnage-sur-Loire. The village about which there are no stories does not exist.

The two model-makers wandered round the village and looked into the two or three cafés the place contained. They did not see him and did not think it wise to ask for him, and the church clock struck ten.

"This is no use," said Campbell. "Either he is back at the hotel by now or in somebody's private house. Let's go back."

But Hambledon was not in any of the public rooms at the hotel nor yet in his own bedroom.

"Curse the fellow," said Campbell. "I never met his equal for sitting happily nattering for hours to previously total strangers. He is probably discussing religion with the curé. Forgan, I've been thinking."

"Go on," said Forgan. They were in their own sitting-room by then; he took a bottle of wine and two glasses from a cupboard and set them on the table.

"I am wondering whether we really want to stop this stunt tonight or whether it wouldn't be better to let them carry on with it and see where they go."

"You mean, set the police on them and have them followed, do you?"

"No. They'd notice that at once. We might just as well turn up and say 'Desist!' as that." Campbell relapsed into silence and Forgan poured the wine.

"Here's yours."

"Thank you. Cheers! Forgan, where does Arthur keep that waterproof sheet thing he ties over the luggage when it's on the roof of the Rolls?"

"It's in the trunk. I saw it yesterday."

"Good. I think I will be the luggage on the roof of the Rolls."

"But, Campbell——"

"All dressed up in my new bathing suit, looking madder than any hatter ever knew how to be, with my hair on end. I will take a blanket—no, the rug out of the car will do—and if I am dis-

106

covered, surely I can sleep on the roof of my own car if I want to, dammit!"

"But——"

"But the chances are that if they do notice a hump on the roof they'll think nothing of it if the cover is over it well tied down. They're not interested in the car, they only want to borrow it for a few hours."

"I don't like this scheme much, Campbell."

"Then suggest a better. And don't suggest your taking my place on the roof under the cover. They wouldn't think you were luggage, they'd think the car was running on producer gas and you were the bag."

"That's horribly rude," said Forgan, laughing. "Will you take a gun?"

"Yes, I'd better. No, I don't think I will. I think it would destroy that look of innocent lunacy which is my best line of defence. If I take a gun I might as well go out in this suit. What's the time? Nearly half-past ten, I must be changing." Campbell emptied his glass and stood up. "You might perhaps see if Hambledon has come in, if you don't mind."

But Hambledon was still not to be found, and Forgan returned to their rooms. As he closed the sitting-room door behind him, a figure came to Campbell's bedroom door which stopped him in his tracks.

"Campbell! Have you any sort of an idea what you look like?"

"Not really. There's a long glass in your wardrobe door, I'll go in there and look at myself. I think it should be——Great Scott! Marvellous. The worse the better, you know. Now, if I ruffle up my hair, so——"

Forgan covered his eyes.

"What's the matter with you? I'm perfectly respectable, am I not? Now, if I were wearing a Bikini you'd have something to fuss about. Forgan, lend me that big clasp knife of yours; it's got a shackle on the end and I might get a chance to cut that poor victim free. What's his name? Dupont, yes. Where's my nice dog chain I sometimes trail for the dog I haven't got on the end? Thank you, Forgan. I look like the mayor of Loonyville now and this is my chain of office. So. Now the car keys, I shall want the one for the trunk at once and, later, who knows? Forgan, I have a feeling that tonight is going to be fun."

"You can't go through the hotel like that."

"Certainly not. I shall go out of my housemaid's window. I mean, my housemaid's cupboard window. She, wise girl, lives in the village. Look out and see if the passage is clear, Forgan."

"I am coming too——"

"Then you'll go through the hotel. You might get down my way, but you'd never get back. What's the time? A quarter to eleven. I'm off, I must get into position before they start bumbling round. Meet you down by the garages and let's hope nobody sees us. Is anyone about?"

Ten minutes later two dim figures met near the line of garages. They were both adept at moving unnoticeably about; they both wore silent rubber-soled shoes and both used such caution that at the moment of meeting they startled each other. Campbell patted his chest and murmured: "Sit still, my heart! Anybody about?"

"Not down here," answered Forgan in the same low tone. It was a very dark night, and the only sound at the moment was a light wind stirring the leaves. They slid quickly across the front of two lock-up doors and found number three unlocked as promised. They slipped inside and closed the door after them.

Forgan opened the car door and, flicking a torch on for a moment behind the seat, got out the rug. One more momentary flash, carefully screened, showed him the petrol gauge.

"Seven eighths full," he commented. "Arthur must have filled her up."

"Not necessarily," said Campbell, "the needle's stuck again at seven eighths. Come round here a minute with that torch of yours, I can't get the key in this lock. Ah, thank you. Wrong key, that may possibly explain my difficulty. Now."

The trunk opened and disclosed a spare wheel, a kit of tools in a canvas roll, a large brown canvas sheet folded up, and two petrol cans. Campbell tried their weight.

"Full," he said, "both of them. Arthur is learning prudence." He drew out the canvas sheet, which had eyelets and cords at intervals along sides and ends, and relocked the trunk. The keys were with the clasp knife, on the end of the dog chain; Campbell dropped them inside his garment.

"You climb up," said Forgan, "and I'll hand up the rest. Rug first, got it? I'll spread the canvas for you——"

"But I'll tie the strings," said Campbell. "Too, too baffling if I couldn't descend because the knots were out of reach. Take your torch, I shan't want it."

"I shall tell Hambledon," said Forgan, "the moment he comes in. I'll wait to see you drive off."

"There's a nice clump of bushes opposite," said Campbell, tying the last knot. "You'd better go, the time's getting on."

The garage door opened softly and closed again; a few minutes later the clump of bushes opposite waved a little more than was justified by the light wind.

A quarter of an hour later two men came down the path from the hotel to the garages and went in to number three. The car lights were switched on and Forgan could see that the younger of the two men was in the driver's seat while the elder stood by, watching proceedings. Presently the Rolls engine started and began to purr quietly after the manner of Rolls; the elder man, he whom Campbell had called Brown from the colour of his shoes, came out and opened the second garage door. The Rolls emerged with dignity and Brown shut the doors behind it; as he did so Forgan saw him glance interestedly at the roof. Presumably Black saw it too, for he put his head out of the window and asked: "What is it?"

"Luggage on the roof," said Brown in tones inaudible to Forgan but which rose clearly to Campbell, "and you keep your thieving fingers off it. Very good camouflage, for who would suspect a car of this type with luggage on the roof? I daresay the boss put it there on purpose." He got in beside the driver, and the car turned down the drive and passed from Forgan's sight.

Campbell had arranged himself in such a posture as to be able to see which way they were going. The car turned west but avoided passing through Orleans; they crossed the main Paris–Orleans road north of the city. After that they took a series of winding country lanes only signposted—if at all—with the names of obscure villages which meant nothing to Campbell, though he made a determined effort to memorize the general direction.

At last the car slowed down as though the men inside were looking for a turning; a quarter of a mile later they stopped and

Brown got out to direct, in very low tones, the driver to back up what appeared to be a private entrance; for on the road there was a gate which Brown opened and set wide, and the grass verges of the drive had been neatly scythed. They went some fifty yards till Brown said: "That will do. Stop. Put the lights out."

"Thank goodness for that," said Brown, obeying. "What's the time?"

"Just about one. Nice time. He'll be sound asleep. Come on."

Presumably they went, for Campbell heard no more. He turned over very cautiously, since he did not know how far they had gone or how long they would be away, and told himself that next time he rode on the roof of a car he would provide a mattress rather than a blanket, for Rolls' roofs are hard and this one was ribbed for luggage as well. He tucked several thicknesses of rug between the more salient points of his anatomy and the roof, and settled down to wait again.

After what seemed a long time he heard quite definite footsteps of someone who was not wearing crepe-rubber soles. The steps were uneven and shuffling and conveyed a definite sense of unwillingness to participate.

"Come on!" said Brown's voice, hushed but recognizable. "I don't care if I do cut your throat and leave you. At last! Now lash his legs, Michel."

More scuffling and a muttered imprecation.

"Now," said Brown, "drop him in the back, on the floor. That's right." The sound of a door shutting. "Now, drive as fast as you like."

"Not on these roads," said Michel, alias Black. "If I was to ditch her we'd be sunk."

Two doors closed, the car engine started again, and they moved off down the drive into the lane and back the way they had come.

"And if I had the faintest idea where St. Antoine's was," said Campbell, resting his chin on his crossed arms, "it would be nice."

As far as he could tell, they went back by the way they had come for seven or eight miles and then took a right fork. This part of the journey was certainly fresh, for they passed a farm wagon at the side of the road and he was sure he had not seen it before. A couple of miles further on the Rolls coughed in her genteel manner—one could almost see her putting her hand up—and the engine stopped. Michel coasted to the side of the road and put the brakes on.

"What's the matter?" asked Brown.

"Sounds to me like we've run out of petrol."

"We can't have." Brown turned on the dashlight to see the petrol gauge. "She's nearly full."

"After forty-five miles? Don't be silly. The needle's stuck, that's what." Michel gave the dial a thump with a gloved hand; the needle started nervously and flicked back to zero. "There you are. Of all the—— What do we do now?"

"There might be some in the trunk," said Brown, getting out and walking round the car. "It's locked. Give me the ignition key, perhaps it fits both locks."

Campbell smiled to himself.

"It doesn't," said Brown's voice after a pause. "It won't even go in."

"Didn't suppose it would," said Michel in a voice gone squeaky with rage and frustration. "I thought you said your boss was something wonderful. Must be, to send us out on a job like this with a tank all but empty. I suppose if he was here he'd just say 'Go' and the car would go, eh? Of all the——"

"Stop that," said Brown sharply. "You're getting hysterical."

"What's the penalty for kidnapping? Fifteen years in a penal settlement?"

There was a momentary silence and then, from somewhere near at hand, a cock crew.

"Hear that?" said Brown. "There's a farm just along the road here. Sure to be petrol there. Come on, we'll go and get it."

"What in?"

"There's always buckets round a farm. You'd better come too; you can hold the torch."

"Borrow a horse and tow her," grumbled Michel, but he fell in beside Brown and the two walked away along the road. Campbell untied enough of the cover lashings to enable him to sit up, and waited for a few minutes more.

Ahead of the car, a hundred yards away, the torch lit up the gable end of a barn and then went off the road.

Campbell threw his legs over the side of the car and swung himself down; the next moment he had the trunk open and was lifting out one of the cans with precautions against making a noise. Sounds carry on a still night, but Brown and Black, however quick their ears, would not hear the refreshing gurgle of petrol swishing into the empty tank.

"That'll take us home," said Campbell, replacing the can and shutting the trunk all in one movement. He ran round to the driver's seat and was in the act of getting in when he paused to look over into the back. He could only see dimly that there was something on the floor, but it did not move or speak, and a horrible conviction seized upon Campbell that it was already dead or dying. He shot out again, opened the back door, and dragged Monsieur Dupont into the road.

His hands were lashed together and his arms to his sides, more cords bound his ankles and knees, and there was a pillow case over his head.

Campbell opened his knife and cut the lashings on arms and legs. Dupont moved feebly and made a bubbling noise, so Campbell picked him up bodily, propped him against the rear fender, and ripped off the pillow case to reveal its contents.

Monsieur Dupont was short and fat; he had a round red face, a spiky moustache, and hair that stood up like a feather mop, though this last effect was probably due to the pillow case. He was wearing formal city clothes, a dress which made his extreme dishevelment proportionately shocking. He did not attempt to move or look up, and Campbell thought him dazed with fright.

"Come," began Campbell, "if you will get into the car——"

Dupont looked up and saw plainly, in the light of the rear lamp, the apparition which had startled even Forgan. It wore a frightful striped garment, its red hair stood up round its head like flames, and in its hand it held a gleaming knife.

Dupont uttered one frightful yell of terror, sprang across the road through a wide gap opposite, and ran like a hare. Campbell instinctively started after him, but the little man had vanished in the darkness.

"That yell's done it," said Campbell. He leapt for the driving seat and started the Rolls. Along at the farm a wavering light could be seen; there came to his ears a distant clatter as of one who falls over a pail, and instantly dogs began to bark. Campbell turned the car into the gap in the hedge, meaning to back out, but when he found that he was on firm pasture he circled the car in the field and came out again. By this time a bobbing light was coming up the lane and shots were fired as he turned away. They did not hit the Rolls nor, probably, Dupont, but they had a moral effect upon him, for a fresh outburst of cries signified his distress and faded rapidly away in the distance.

"You may be fat," said Campbell aloud, "but I'll tell the world you can run."

He put his foot down and drove as fast as the road permitted. He turned left and left again; ten minutes later, by pure luck, he came upon the Paris–Orleans road and crossed it into country that he knew.

Three quarters of an hour later he was berthing the Rolls in its own garage at Arnage-sur-Loire.

CHAPTER 12 *Boiled Mussels*

MONSIEUR PEYRET, journalist of the *Orleans Intelligencer*, had also been up all night. Ever since the Juge d'Instruction's enquiry into the death of Alan Power at Arnage, Peyret had been in bad odour with his editor. Peyret had had the sparkling initiative, according to himself or the blazing insolence, according to his editor, to telephone direct to Exchange Telegraph and Central News in London and tell them that an Englishman had been foully slain by an unknown assassin. The editor did not wish to dismiss Peyret since he was a bright young man with a nose for news, but he was, the editor considered, getting too big for his boots and should be reduced. The process consisted in sending out Peyret on every tiresome, uninspiring assignment which came into the office, and if there was a downpour of rain at the time, so much the better.

Peyret had retired to bed just after midnight after attending a dinner of the Anciens Camarades de la Guerre, whose speeches might just as well have been reported from last year's notes, as they always said the same things. At three in the morning his telephone rang and transmitted the voice of his editor telling him to go at once to a place on the further side of Montargis, where the country house of a celebrated general—name given— was said to be in flames. Peyret could take the office car and should be on the road in ten minutes.

He was on the road in twenty minutes, and when he reached the place he found that the celebrated general's house was not even in danger because the fire was busily destroying a row of cottages half a mile down the road. Nobody was hurt and the inhabitants had even salvaged most of their possessions. No news value at all. Peyret yawned, rubbed his eyes, which were stinging

114

with smoke and want of sleep, and turned the car in the road to go back to Orleans and bed. The road was narrow, the night was darker than ever just before the dawn, and there was a ditch behind him which he did not see. He was backing the car carefully when it suddenly slid back and sat down with its rear wheels in eighteen inches of liquid mud and its headlights pointing foolishly at the fading stars.

Nobody could be bothered to help him; they were all busy running about with pails of water. Horse? There was no horse there; these smoking ruins were houses, not stables. There would be horses later on, at a Christian hour in the morning.

Peyret asked himself yet once more why he had been such a fool as to take up journalism instead of accepting the good position offered to him by his uncle, the undertaker, crawled into the front seat of his car, and went to sleep.

He reached the *Intelligencer* office at Orleans at about half-past nine, having breakfasted at Montargis, and reported that the fire was a complete flop and that the general had not even been disturbed. The editor said that that did not now matter at all as something much more promising had broken; a well-known businessman had disappeared from his home. Monsieur Alcimène Dupont, of the well-known firm of Dupont, Dulac et Cie., Iron Founders, of Paris, had left his country home in the middle of the night and no one knew where he had gone. "It's a big firm," said the editor, "and there have been rumours going round that it is a bit shaky. The shares have been dropping slowly for the past week or so; this news will send them down with a run. I am glad to say I don't hold any. If Dupont has skipped, which is possible, this might be a big story. I have already got his photograph out of the files, just in case." the editor picked up a photograph of Dupont from his desk, glanced at it, and threw it down again; Peyret screwed his head round sideways to see it and took a mental note of the round fat face, the small spiky black moustache, and the general effect of neat prosperity. "You had better go to his house— here's the address—and see if you can pick up anything. Take the office car. That is all."

"At once, monsieur," said Peyret alertly, and dashed out of the office. Once in the car, he drove straight to his lodgings for a bath, a shave, a change of clothes, since he had slept in his suit and it looked it, and another breakfast, after which he drove off to The Nest, for such was the name which Dupont had deliberately chosen for his country cottage. Dupont had desired a quiet rural retreat remote from passing traffic or local excitements and had found it so successfully that intending visitors very often could not find it at all. Peyret lost his way in the lanes.

He arrived eventually at Le Nid a little after one and was not at all kindly received. Quite the contrary. The door was answered by a harassed manservant in a black alpaca jacket who looked as though something had annoyed him; when Peyret with his most winning smile presented his card, he found out what it was.

"A journalist? Another journalist! *Sainte Vierge*, I have spent the whole morning beating off journalists with broom handles! Since nine o'clock they are here, sometimes two or three at once. Where is Monsieur Dupont? I say, if I knew that he would not be missing. When did he go—why did he go—did he leave a message —did I know he was going—where did I think him likely to have gone—did he take a suitcase—did he have breakfast—was he subject to loss of memory—dizziness—spots before the eyes—had he ever done this before? Mother of Heaven I don't know, I don't know, I don't know, and my wife, she has hysterics—GO AWAY!"

The door slammed with such violence that one of a row of small panes of glass fell out and tinkled to fragments at Peyret's feet. Locks were ostentatiously turned and bolts loudly shot; as Peyret stood there hesitating a segment of an angry face appeared in the square from which the glass had fallen and bellowed: "Go away!"

"Some people," said Peyret, turning back to his car, "don't like publicity. What a day. Now I drive back to Orleans without a story and the Old Man'll have my head off. What a day!"

He recovered his cheerfulness as he drove along the lanes, for it was not in Peyret to be discouraged for long, and began to compose in his mind a really sparkling account of his reception at Le Nid. The right words presented themselves in the right order; witty and well-balanced sentences unrolled themselves without effort. "I shall get something out of this after all," he thought, and then had to cram his brakes on suddenly to avoid a man who staggered out of the hedge right in his path. The man looked round at him and began very unsteadily and waveringly to run away. He was fat and had a round red face with a small spiky moustache; he was wearing a neat city suit, but it looked as though he had been rolling in it; he was——

Peyret leaped out of the car and ran after him. "Monsieur Dupont! Please stop, Monsieur Dupont! Can I help you in any way?"

Dupont stopped, swaying on his feet; he looked to be in the last stages of exhaustion.

"Who are you—do not touch me——"

"Peyret, of the *Orleans Intelligencer*, monsieur. Here is my card. Can I perhaps drive you——"

Dupont staggered and caught at Peyret's arm for support.

"To the police, at once, the nearest police station without the least delay."

"Immediately, monsieur. Let me assist Monsieur into my car— there. Let Monsieur relax himself, all is now well."

"To the police," said Dupont, "to the police." He leaned back and closed his eyes.

"By the most direct route, monsieur." Peyret sprang into the driving seat and drove on. Darkness had turned to light; single-handed he had brought off the scoop of a lifetime. His only trouble now was that he wanted to sing and had a strong feeling that it would not be tactful. He glanced at Dupont, who stirred weakly and murmured: "To the police."

"At my best speed, monsieur."

Five minutes later he glanced down again, and this time Dupont was asleep.

The car swirled through the streets of Orleans, and Dupont woke up as Peyret stopped before a tall building and sprang out to help his passenger to alight.

"Is this the police station?" he asked thickly.

"In at this door, monsieur, and up this flight of stairs. Let Monsieur lean on my arm and also take hold of the handrail. So. Let Monsieur take his time."

Together they walked slowly up the stairs; they traversed a long corridor where passing colleagues stared curiously at Peyret's companion; together they reached a door at the far end at which Peyret knocked. His great moment had arrived.

"*Entrez!*"

"Monsieur," said Peyret with simple pride, "it is my privilege and honour to present to you Monsieur Alcimène Dupont of Messieurs Dupont, Dulac et Cie. of Paris." He led his patient forward and said: "Let me get Monsieur a chair. He has——"

The editor himself leapt from his chair, swept a pile of papers from the padded armchair kept for the use of Very Distinguished Visitors only, and wheeled it up behind Dupont.

"I beg Monsieur to be seated. Let Monsieur——"

"I want the police."

"They shall be sent for," said the editor magnificently. "Monsieur has a complaint to make?" He went back to his place and laid his hand upon the telephone without, of course, any intention of lifting it until he had heard the story himself.

"Tell them that I, Alcimène Dupont, have been abducted by armed savages, forced to dress and creep out of my own house in silence, bound hand and foot and a bag forced over my head, thrust into the back of a car driven I know not where, dragged out again and my bonds removed by a maniac with flaming hair who threatened me with a large knife. I want some coffee," he added abruptly.

The editor put his finger on the bell and kept it there until a boy rushed in.

"Coffee," said the editor. "Hot and strong."

"Fresh also," said Dupont. "The best coffee."

"You heard," said the editor to the messenger, who instantly fled.

"Peyret," said the editor, "you have heard this story?"

"Not a word, monsieur. When I found Monsieur Dupont he was too exhausted to speak."

Dupont was recovering rapidly in a friendly and deferential atmosphere where his wishes were instantly obeyed.

"Young man," he said, "you have done me a service and I am deeply in your debt. Alcimène Dupont does not forget those who have obliged him."

"My staff," put in the editor, "are under the strictest orders to be helpful and obliging to any who are in trouble. For all recompense, tell us, monsieur, I beg, your story in the fullest detail." He nodded to Peyret, who sat down in a corner and took out his notebook.

"Last night," began Dupont, "I retired to bed at my usual hour——"

(Extract from the files of the *Orleans Intelligencer.*)

M. Alcimène Dupont, Chairman and Managing Director of the well-known firm of Dupont, Dulac et Cie. of Paris, has been the victim of an unprecedented and inexplicable outrage, as remarkable for its daring and brutality as for the bizarre and fantastic details of its execution. M. Dupont, still pale and shaken from the ordeal through which he had so lately passed and from which he was finally rescued by a member of the *Intelligencer* staff, sat in our office and told us the following story.

He had come out to his country cottage, Le Nid, for a few days' rest and to think over some business matter which awaited his decision. Last night—Wednesday—he retired to rest at his usual time and fell asleep at once, only to be awakened soon after one by someone shaking his shoulder and shining a light into his eyes. At once a harsh but low-toned voice forbade him to speak or cry out upon peril of being instantly shot dead, and a gun was held to his head. He was then ordered to get up and dress himself, an order which he dared not to disobey. He was led down the stairs and out of the house. Once upon the drive of his charming little property, his hands were tied together, his arms bound to his sides, and he was made to walk along the drive to where a large car was waiting. Here his knees and ankles were similarly bound with cords, a bag was forced over his head, and he was roughly thrown into the back of the car, upon the floor. The car was then drove off.

Some time later the car stopped again and there was some talk between his captors about petrol.

They got out of the car. A few moments later M. Dupont heard a scrambling noise and, soon after, what he took to be the sound of petrol being poured into the tank. Very shortly after that, someone dragged him out of the car, cut his bonds, and pulled off the bag which had covered his head.

It is at this point that M. Dupont's story abandons the normal account of such crimes of violence as too often evade the vigilance of our excellent police and becomes a *Grand Guignol* narrative of madness, knives, and horror. In the light from the tail lamp of the car, M. Dupont saw facing him a figure which for macabre fantasy far exceeded such blood-chilling fabrications as Dracula or the worst excesses of the American so-called comic strips. The figure was clad in a tight-fitting garment of wide horizontal stripes; upon its head the hair, which was itself the colour of flame, stood upright, writhing and quivering as though each hair were possessed of an infernal vitality of its own; the face, which was large and hairless, bore an expression of subhuman malignity, and the wide-open mouth was wreathed into a fiendish grin. As though this were not enough, the figure held in its hand a large open knife which it slowly raised in the air as though about to plunge it into the body of M. Alcimène Dupont.

M. Dupont says that at this point terror lent wings to his feet. He crossed the road with a single bound, burst through the hedge upon the opposite side, and ran for his life. For our part, we frankly admit that had we been in his place we should, if possible, have run even faster. M. Dupont considers that he was abducted in order to be the victim of some hellish rite of human sacrifice. Fantastic as this suggestion may appear, it is alas not impossible. Such cults have risen before and may rise again. We need only instance etc., etc.

Hambledon, having already heard Campbell's account of the night's proceedings, laughed over this until the tears ran down his face. He then departed in haste for Paris, taking the *Orleans Intelligencer* with him for Letord's delectation, and Letord stood him a lunch on the strength of it.

"But your so ingenious assistant," said Letord, "will have to send away or destroy his beautiful garment. This article"—he tapped the paper—"will be read by all in the district, and thus your conspirators will know, if they see the garment, who was responsible for their downfall that night. We do not wish to lose the services of so resourceful a man."

"I have already told him so," said Hambledon. "Tell me about Dupont, will you?"

"Certainly. Dupont, Dulac et Cie. started in a small way and are now large and efficient. That is, Dupont is efficient. He is the firm; Dulac was some relation who put money into it and is now dead. There were rumours going the rounds that the firm was financially shaky, no proof adduced, you understand, but always the whispers. Dupont heard about them and was both frightened and furious; he even asked advice from a colleague of mine who specializes in financial investigations, but what could he advise? But if this scheme had succeeded and Monsieur Dupont had disappeared for a few days, everyone would have said that he had bolted with what was left of the firm's money and the shares would have gone right down to the bottom of all things. Then your conspirators buy, of course. Later Dupont is released and it is plain that the whole scheme was a swindle from the start and that there is nothing wrong with the firm after all. So once again the shares rise to their normal level, your conspirators sell their bargains and reap a nice profit. It was not a big affair, not like those television shares I told you about, the ones that nearly ruined the Bank of Monaco. I think, myself, that on that occasion they overreached themselves; it was a little too big, eh? So they try something more manageable; what is that saying you have in England? Small profits and quick returns, is it?"

"I am glad to notice that you agree with me," said Hambledon, "that this Dupont business is all part of the big conspiracy, as Power called it. He——"

"But, naturally! It is the same method used to the same ends!"

"And Power was right in another matter; it is being worked from Arnage. It is being worked from my hotel. These men were ordered to go there to receive instructions over the room telephones, and it would be quite impossible for them—or anyone else—to discover from which room the instructions came. One does not ring up the office and ask to be put through to room so-and-so; one just dials the number direct. Ideal for their purpose."

"It need not be," pursued Letord, "anyone connected with the hotel at all; it could equally as well be a visitor. I see. I think you have something on your plate there, my friend. Of course we will hunt for your two men; one of them we know, and we have your and Vidal's descriptions of the other. But, if I were they, I would not be still in France. Eh?"

Hambledon agreed. "There is another matter you might look into. St. Antoine's."

"St. Antoine's what? Café? Wine cellars? Castle? Cottage? Or even a soubriquet for some man because he is allergic to the ladies, eh? Our St. Antoine, he is very popular as a name if not so popular as an example. However, I will look, though I do not know where or for what. It is hampering, that. Well now, you have told me one funny story, now I tell you one in exchange. The Spider is missing."

"The Spider—what, that private enquiry agent? Spiders Anonymous, 'we spread webs, we catch men'? Perhaps somebody has caught him."

"Perhaps." Letord began to laugh. "It is unkind to be amused —the poor man may be in trouble—but it is funny for all that. They think themselves so good, you know? We are the mutton-headed police and they run rings round us every time, and now —I tell you about it. The Spider, Jean Jaboulet, has a head clerk, I told you. Only yesterday he came to me and said the Spider was missing, would I please find him for them. Always when he is away he telephones his office at least once a week and usually more often, but now he is gone for three weeks without a word. I said, but your so clever young men, why not send them out to find him? But the head clerk says they have been searching now these several days without the least success, so will we take a hand?" Letord laughed again, but Hambledon was not so greatly amused.

"The Spider was looking into this conspiracy business too, was he not, on behalf——"

"You are right, of course, I told you that myself. He was engaged by Julius Aldebert to prove that the death of his brother Marius Aldebert was murder and not suicide. That was the case which set your man Power on the track of all this. Yes, the head clerk admitted that that was what the Spider was doing and he said he was looking into another matter also, Madame Rougisson's idea that her husband was away with another woman, you remember? And not in North Africa watching bird migration."

"But," said Hambledon incredulously, "but the head of a firm like that—a man who thought so much of himself—to snoop round himself collecting smutty evidence of marital infidelity? Nonsense, Letord, nonsense. He would send his latest-joined recruit on that job. It is as though you ran round the streets of Paris detecting parking offences."

"I should not have to run far," said Letord sourly. "But there is something in what you say. It is odd, that."

"There is always something in what I say," protested Hambledon. "But if the Spider was really shadowing Rougisson, do you suppose that he also was at Arnage?"

"Perhaps, when you go back, you will find his corpse under your bed," said Letord. "Now, when you were here last, you became interested in a certain Café de Bruges, you remember? Yes. So I had it looked up in records, and this is all we know about it.

"At one time the Café de Bruges was kept by a man named Tiffet and his wife. The place had not a good name although it was kept orderly enough, but it was the resort of criminals and their associates, and for that reason we, the police, kept an eye on it. About three years ago a riot broke out there one night; it was quite serious in a small way. The criminals quarrelled over something, I suppose, and fought each other with anything which came to hand; there was a deal of damage done and windows were broken—you know. We were not called in, so we did not interfere; for me, if these assassins knife each other I do not shed tears. No. After it was all over Madame Tiffet came to us and said that her husband was missing since that night; that she herself did not see anything because she had rushed upstairs and barricaded herself in her bedroom but that someone had seen him being set on in a corner by several at once and after that he had not been seen at all. We looked for him but we did not even find his corpse; myself, I think it is probably still in the Seine. So after a time she was given leave to presume death and the café became hers. There has been no trouble whatever since, and criminals no longer frequent it, so we have lost interest in the place. They tell me it is a quiet dull place now, and that is all I know, my friend."

Hambledon thanked him and took his leave. The Café de Bruges did not sound very interesting, a grubby little place which had suffered a disturbance three years ago and behaved itself ever since. However, Power had its telephone number; it was worth while going to look at it. It is not far from the Île de la Cité to the Bastille area, and Hambledon walked up to the Rue de l'Arbre Vert.

He found the Café de Bruges to be much as he expected to find it; a door and one wide window, blistered paint of a medium shade of mud on the ground floor and none at all on the windows above. The pavement outside was grimy and had a permanent stain across it from a leaking down-pipe; orange peel and scraps of paper lay in the gutter. Across the window was written in a large decorative hand in whitening, *Specialité de la Maison. moules. Pommes Frites*, with flourishes between the words.

Hambledon remembered the odd passion which the Belgians indulge for boiled mussels and fried potatoes; presumably whoever named the café had called it after his home town. He shuddered slightly but pushed open the door and went in.

The place was not exactly dirty nor precisely clean; it held a variety of smells which Hambledon carefully refrained from identifying. By the door there was the statutory framed licence announcing that the Café de Bruges was under the proprietorship of Mlle. Alphonsine Buchot of the same address. Not Tiffet, so presumably the place had changed hands. However, he went up the central passage, between small square tables with chairs set about them, to the bar at the far end and asked for a *grand fine*. The woman who served him was large and stout, of any age between thirty and fifty, in a grubby flowered overall. She was civil enough, but her face was without animation or interest, and Hambledon found the most desultory conversation difficult to maintain. He sipped his cognac and looked about him.

There were some half dozen people in the place and two of them were eating mussels alternately with fried potatoes. Even as he looked an elderly man came in, nodded to the woman behind the bar, and sat down at a table by himself. The woman called some order through an adjacent doorway. A few moments later there emerged the very oldest waiter Hambledon had ever seen; he looked eighty at the least. He staggered out under the weight of a metal tureen full to the top of steaming mussels, carried it down to the elderly man's table, and returned to the kitchen. A moment later he was back with a vegetable dish piled with thinly sliced golden-hued fried potatoes.

Hambledon finished his cognac and beat a retreat.

CHAPTER 13 *The Corpse Says No*

BEFORE DINNER that evening Hambledon was sitting up at the bar in the lounge of the Hotel de la Poste sipping a glass of Tio Pepe and engaging in desultory conversation with the bartender and a Dutchman who was staying in the hotel. There were only some half dozen people in the lounge since most of the company had already gone in to dinner, but one of them was Detective Sergeant Vidal, who was sitting quietly in a corner finishing one of his handmade cigarettes and looking through *Paris Illustré*. Forgan and Campbell had already gone up to the private room where their meals were served. It was a peaceful, placid scene.

A few minutes later Vidal stubbed out his cigarette, threw down the paper, and got to his feet; he nodded to Hambledon in passing and turned in the passage leading to the dining-room. At that moment the swing doors of the hotel entrance were flung open and a man stamped in and came to a dramatic stop, staring angrily about him. He was a middle-aged man with dark hair and a bristling dark beard going grey; he was untidily though not shabbily dressed in the sort of thing which France produces when asked for country clothes; a tweed jacket, plus-fours, thick knitted stockings, and heavy shoes. The shoes were not only smeared with dry mud but had plainly not been polished for some time, and his hair stood up in tufts, as though he had been running his fingers through it. He had in one hand a folded newspaper which he shook occasionally as though it annoyed him.

Since he was a total stranger to everyone present, no one spoke to him and there was a general hush eventually broken by the stranger himself.

"I want the manager," he said in a loud harsh voice.

126

Gallet shot out of the manager's office. "Monsieur?"

"Are you the manager? I have come to make a complaint about this ridiculous article in this nasty little paper." He shook out the newspaper which he held in his hand, and Hambledon recognized it as a copy of the *Orleans Intelligencer*. "This damned rag says I'm dead. Murdered, in fact, here in this so-called hotel. How dare you say I'm dead?"

"Monsieur," stammered Gallet, "monsieur, please. I have not even the honour of knowing Monsieur's name."

"All France knows it," said the stranger magnificently. "I am Raoul Rougisson, the ornithologist. Now will you say you have never heard it?"

If there had been silence before, there was absolute stillness now. No one moved, no one spoke; one would have said that no one breathed; as for Gallet, he might have been turned into one of those life-sized waxen-faced tailors' models which in any case he rather resembled. One slight movement caught the tail of Hambledon's eye, and he looked round to see the lean form and dark beaky face of Detective Sergeant Vidal coming to anchor against a corner of the passage from the dining-room. The stranger looked round at seven or eight amazed faces and lost his temper.

"What the devil's the matter with you all? Do you take me for a ghost?"

"But, yes, monsieur——"

" 'But, yes, monsieur,' " mimicked the stranger. "Fool! Idiot! Nincompoop! Look at this." He thrust the *Orleans Intelligencer* under Gallet's nose and indicated, with a stabbing forefinger, one of the columns. "There, look. Not that, that's a dab of butter. It came round the groceries."

There was a moment's pause while Gallet concentrated on the paper, and Hambledon's Dutch friend remarked in a low quivering voice that he would not have missed this for ten thousand guilders.

"I have, naturally, seen this before," said Gallet. "It is a true account of a tragedy which took pl——"

"It is not true! It says it is I! I mean, that I am he and I am not, I tell you. I demand that——"

Vidal detached himself from the corner against which he had been leaning and crossed the lounge.

"Monsieur, if you please. My name is Vidal and I am the detective sergeant in charge of the investigations into the murder of Raoul Rougisson."

"Then you can call yourself off and go home if you have one. No, first you can officially contradict this ridiculous story and then go home. Murdered! Me? Do I look it? Do I sound as though I were dead?"

"No indeed, monsieur," said Vidal calmly. "I am quite sure that monsieur is most completely alive, but that does not—forgive me—prove that Monsieur is the celebrated Raoul Rougisson. No doubt Monsieur has his identity papers with him?"

The stranger paused for a moment. "No, I have not my papers with me at the moment. That is, they were not in the pockets of this suit—I saw this monstrous slander in the paper—I rushed straight off——"

"Unfortunate," said Vidal. "Particularly unfortunate, since it seems that Monsieur has come here expressly to contest a question of identity."

The stranger reddened. "If you must know, they were stolen from me—what—over a fortnight ago. There was a damned persistent fellow came to the house trying to sell things——"

"No doubt Monsieur instantly informed the police as required by law?"

"Well, no. The fact is, I was on holiday in a place miles from any police station. I did not want my papers there; I thought it would do when I returned——"

"With the result," said Vidal, "that Monsieur has now no proofs of identity to show. The police, as Monsieur doubtless knows, would have given him duplicates at once, particularly if Monsieur's story were supported by the testimony of his friends."

For some reason this harmless remark appeared to have hit the stranger in a sensitive spot, for he actually recoiled, and at that moment the telephone rang. It was the telephone on the reception desk in the lounge, and Gallet lifted the receiver.

"Hotel de la Poste, Arnage-sur-Loire . . . I beg your pardon, what name? . . . Just a moment, please."

He covered the mouthpiece with one hand, looked at Vidal, and said: "A lady asking for Monsieur Rougisson."

"That's for me," said the stranger, and strode across the lounge.

"Let him have it," said Vidal agreeably.

"Allô, allô, allô," said the stranger into the mouthpiece. "Yes, of course I have, *chérie*, or I shouldn't be here, should I? . . . Yes. No, well, I have not been here long enough to—— What? . . . Yes, of course I will, as soon as possible. . . . There's five thousand francs in my dressing case if you look. . . . Five thousand, yes . . . Listen, *chérie*, surely you can make that—— What? But I paid him. . . . I don't know. It makes it very awkward, not having my papers that fellow . . . Yes, of course I'll be as quick as I . . . Listen, *chérie*, it's a question . . . Listen, a question of proving identity, and I don't know anybody here. . . . No, certainly not. *Mon Dieu*, no! I absolutely forbid . . . Don't be a fool! You know what . . . I say, you know what my wife . . ."

He was getting more and more excited; he took short agitated steps about the reception desk. Gallet seized the telephone instrument at the moment when it was about to be dragged off the desk to fall on the floor, and followed the speaker round with it like an earnest acolyte offering incense.

"You just stay quiet where you are," continued the stranger. "Yes, I daresay it is dull, but surely . . . Listen. In my opinion five thousand francs is quite a lot of . . ."

Hambledon's Dutch acquaintance leaned his head against Hambledon's shoulder and made small snuffling noises.

"Yes, of course I'll send . . . What? No, not to Paris. You little fool, haven't you the brains of a rabbit? Go wherever you like, but not to Paris. . . . Go to hell!" The stranger banged down the receiver on the bracket offered, at full stretch of the flex, by the attentive Gallet and turned away, wiping his forehead. "*Mon Dieu*, these women!"

He came face to face with Vidal's expression, at once cynical, amused, and faintly sympathetic, and reddened again. Everyone else in the lounge immediately pretended to be interested in something else, and Hambledon ordered another sherry for himself and a Bols for his friend, who was openly wiping his eyes.

"Reverting," said Vidal, "to the important question of Monsieur's identity. Has Monsieur no friend in the immediate neighbourhood who could vouch for him?"

The stranger considered. "There is a man I know in Orleans," he said. "Henri Delamere. He's an entomologist. I've known him for years."

"With regret, I fear that Monsieur Delamere is now hardly in a position to testify to Monsieur's identity."

"Why not? Is he dead at last?"

"Oh no. But only four days ago he identified Monsieur's corpse——"

"*What?*"

"I beg a thousand pardons for an inexcusable slip of the tongue. I mean that Monsieur Delamere identified the body which we had here to deal with as being that of Monsieur Raoul Rougisson of Paris, the well-known ornithologist. Under these circumstances we could hardly——"

"Blistering old idiot!"

"——hardly adduce his evidence as reliable if indeed he did recognize the monsieur I now see before me as——"

"Delamere's as blind as a bat, he——"

"——as the same gentleman who so recently he had identified dead."

"He can't see his hand before his face. I myself saw him once take off his hat to a black horse because he thought it was the curé, and when the horse, as it were, nodded at him, as horses do, he said he was a charming fellow."

"Dear me," said Vidal. "Er—excuse me just one short moment ——Monsieur Gallet!"

Gallet sprang to attention. Vidal whispered in his ear and the undermanager nodded and went into the office, shutting the door behind him.

"Calling up reinforcements?" murmured the Dutchman in Hambledon's ear.

"I imagine so."

"In any case," said Vidal, returning to the attack, "it is not far to Paris, and I understand that Madame Rougisson resides——"

"No, no, no. Not my wife, I could not—that is, there are reasons —not my wife. No. Certainly not. Besides, once you refer to Paris, there are plenty of people there who know me without dragging in my wife. She—she wouldn't like it." The stranger mopped his brow. "You don't know my wife. Very—very sensitive woman, my wife."

"But Madame Rougisson has, for nearly a week, been mourning the loss of a husband to whom she was doubtless devoted."

The stranger snorted loudly.

"And for whom," went on Vidal, "she organized obsequies of the most distinguished, with a cortege which included representatives of many learned societies——"

"*Sacré!*"

"And several carriages entirely filled with wreaths. The ceremony took place at Père Lachaise yesterday; there were photographs—— Has anyone a copy of today's *Figaro?*" added Vidal, turning to the enthralled company. "There was one here."

Hambledon passed it to him, and the stranger snatched it. Gallet came out of the office, nodded at Vidal, and mouthed the word "*immédiatement.*"

"But this is an outrage!" stormed the stranger. "Who is this rogue whom you have buried in my name? And who is going to pay for all this"—he stabbed the paper so hard that his finger went through the page—"this unseemly display?"

"May I ask," said Vidal, "where Monsieur has been during the last few days not to have heard of this affair before today?"

The stranger threw down the *Figaro.* "As a matter of fact," he said in an offhand voice, "I was in North Africa. In Morocco, to be precise. Studying bird migration, actually. This paper—the rag I brought with me—it came wrapped round the groceries, to keep the flies off, presumably. Swarms of flies in Morocco. I picked it up idly, as one does, you know—I had not seen a newspaper for days—when to my disgust I saw that ridiculous story about myself. So I rushed off at once, not even waiting to pack my bag, to quash this ludicrous, this insolent, this——"

"Monsieur travelled by——?"

"By air, naturally. I arrived this morning, and——"

"Having no personal papers, it would be interesting to know how Monsieur managed to enter the country."

There was a horrid silence. Eventually the stranger broke into an embarrassed laugh.

"You would bring that up," he said. "Well, to tell you the truth this time——"

"It would be as well," said Vidal coldly.

"I said I was going to North Africa. I said so because I desired a quiet holiday free from interruptions. In point of fact I was staying with friends."

The swing doors opened. Maroche walked in, saluted Vidal, and stood at attention waiting for orders.

"The murder of a man hitherto believed to be Monsieur Raoul Rougisson is still a matter for the most stringent enquiry," said Vidal. "That being so, I must inform Monsieur that I am detaining him as a material witness. Maroche——"

"What? But this is an outrage. What? Arrest me? How dare you? What am I supposed to have done to be arrested?"

"Monsieur is not being arrested, merely detained."

"Is this justice? Is this French justice, that a man should be locked up because he dares to protest when he is declared to be dead and buried? Buried! And if anybody supposes that I am going to pay for that mummery he can reconsider it. I won't do it."

"Monsieur has not, I believe, yet been asked to do so. But Monsieur reminds me," said Vidal with his eyebrows going up till they resembled a pair of *accents circonflexes*, "that when he arrives in Paris he will be able to do something not within the power of one in a hundred million of the most distinguished persons."

"What is that?"

"To admire his own funeral wreaths; to study the inscriptions, touching or dignified; to read his obituary notices; to receive the——"

"Bah!" said the stranger, and shuddered visibly.

"Maroche."

"*Mon sergent?*"

"Take Monsieur to your place while I ring up Orleans to send a car. Monsieur Gallet——"

"One moment," said the stranger.

"Monsieur?"

"In the place where I shall be detained, does one receive telephone calls?"

"If specially desired, monsieur, such as from one's lawyer or one's next of kin."

"Nobody can—er—get at one?"

"Certainly not, monsieur."

"Come," said the stranger to Maroche, "let us go before that infernal tele——"

The telephone bell rang, and Maroche and the stranger passed rapidly through the swing doors so much together that it was impossible to say which was leading which. The call was, however, a matter of hotel business only.

Hambledon saw Letord at the Sûreté on the Quai des Orfèvres the following afternoon, as it was understood that he would be engaged in the morning. When Hambledon was shown in, Letord turned in his swivel chair to greet him.

"My old friend," he said, "when first you came to visit me about this case I said that I always saw you, in my mind, surrounded by a decorative frieze of corpses. Not now. From this morning you will carry with you a strong aura of low comedy. Very low." He stopped to laugh and then went on: "You have not met Madame Rougisson, no?"

"No, thank you," said Hambledon politely.

"My friend, you are wrong. You miss there something unbelievable. I tell you. The Orleans police brought Monsieur Rougisson to me this morning at ten hours, here in this room, and he tells me his story. The truth, I think, but there is still the official identification to be made. So at half-past ten Madame Rougisson is shown in." He laughed again.

"One of your famous confrontations. Did you warn the lady?"

"No. Why? She no longer——"

"One of these days, Letord, you'll do this to someone who gasps, turns blue, and falls down dead."

"I have. He was a murderer, he killed a man in the dark and it was not the man he meant to kill, but he did not know that. So when he walked in here and saw the man he thought was dead— phoo! Just as you describe. It saved a lot of trouble, for I am not sure that we could have convicted him. No motive, you see. I will tell you the story someday. But Madame Rougisson did not even faint. She stopped short, stared at him, and said: 'Go away, you tiresome creature. You're dead.'"

"God bless my soul," said Hambledon mildly. "What a way to greet a poor ghost."

"So he thought. He complained about it. He said she ought to be glad to see him back. She looked round at us police and pulled herself together. She went up and embraced him formally and said that a series of shocks had unhinged her composure for the moment, and where had he been? He told his nice little story about North Africa, and she curled her lip and said that she did not know that Issoudun was in North Africa. That was the nearest place to where he was staying."

"So Spiders Anonymous did report to her," said Hambledon.

"No doubt. Well, that caught him where it hurt and he began to bluster. She had dared to have him watched, had she? And so on. Then the party began to warm up. He waved his arms about, she tapped the floor with her foot, and they both forgot that they had an interested audience.

"'Tell me,' he says, 'what fool have you buried in my name at Père Lachaise?'

"'How should I know? I thought it was you.'

"'In my plot! Then the scavengers can dig him up again. And you can pay for it.'

"'So. You think so?'

"'And for the tom-fool funeral, too. If you think I'm going to pay for that, you can think again!'

"'What a fool you are, Raoul. You always were, and——'

"'I refuse absolutely——'

"'You drivelling idiot. If you knew what you've landed yourself in, with your cheap tomcat amours! Did you think I didn't know?'

"'If I have sought congenial friends elsewhere, you have driven me to it with your——'

"'Raoul. You had better stop trying to excuse yourself and consider how you are going to repay the insurance money.'

"'What insurance money? I'm not insured.'

"'Oh yes, you are. I insured you since you obstinately refused to make an adequate provision for my widowhood.'

"'What d'you mean? You're not a widow.'

"'Owing entirely to your own deceitful behaviour, no. I thought I was. So did the insurance company.'

"My dear Hambledon, he made a noise just like a farmyard turkey. '*Que—que—que—que——*' You should have heard him."

"That's all right. I have."

"Then he said: 'You cannot mean they have paid out?'

"'Certainly. Why not?'

"'Then you can pay it back.'

"'Don't be foolish. It was mine and I spent it.'

"'How much, in the devil's name?'

"When she told him, Hambledon, his knees gave way, and if

one of my fellows had not pushed a chair behind him he would have been on the floor, and on my faith I do not wonder. These women—"

"I thought," said Hambledon, "that the insurance company only paid out something on account."

"Only a token payment of five million francs. One tenth, in fact, of the total amount."

Hambledon laughed.

"It did not amuse him, no. I do not think, myself, that she can have spent it all even if she has bought a new car, refurnished the flat, and replaced her wardrobe. Could she? All in a week? It does not matter, she is not our wife. Then he got up and called her a string of names and she went for him and slapped his face. I had them parted, and that was that. An unforgettable scene."

"Which you could have stopped at the outset if you had so desired. All you needed was the identification."

"Was it? Do you remember my telling you that both I and the insurance company wondered whether she had had a finger in the pie when he was thought to have been murdered? Yes. And the man who was murdered was passing as Rougisson, was he not? Believe me, I am still looking at Madame, though it is true that she did not even faint this morning."

"You are a ruthless devil, Letord. By the way, we know now who was buried at Père Lachaise for Rougisson, don't we?"

Letord cocked one eyebrow at Hambledon and said: "Do we?"

"Someone who was on this big case of ours and also on the Rougisson matrimonial troubles—incidentally, that would be why he took on that case, which I said was beneath his dignity; because he wanted to borrow Rougisson's identity. He went down there as a travelling pedlar and stole Rougisson's papers, didn't he? You have those, haven't you? Perfectly genuine, aren't they?"

"They are," said Letord, who had been nodding like a mandarin at each point Hambledon raised. "You say the Spider, I say the Spider. Tomorrow they dig him up and we shall know if we were right."

CHAPTER 14 *Café de Bruges*

As soon as the editor of the *Orleans Intelligencer* had absorbed all the details of Monsieur Alcimène Dupont's kidnapping, he had, naturally, no immediate further use for Monsieur Dupont. Peyret was instructed to drive Monsieur Dupont to the police station, where he was most cordially received and his story listened to with the greatest attention by the Superintendent in person. The Superintendent did not tell Monsieur Dupont that the police already knew a great deal more about his story than he did himself, since Campbell had made a full report to Detective Sergeant Vidal at Arnage that morning. The Superintendent knew why Dupont had been abducted—to send his firm's shares down; who had abducted him—the two men who had booked in at the Hotel de la Poste; and who the fantastic figure was who had let him loose, but there was no need to tell Dupont any of that. The only thing the police did not know was where the kidnappers had gone after thier plans had been ruined. They had vanished.

"There's no news of those fellows," said the Superintendent to Vidal on the following day. "They have not been seen on the roads or on the railways, and nobody has reported a car stolen. It is unfortunate that Monsieur Campbell cannot say exactly where he left them."

"With respect, mon Surintendant, one could hardly expect it. It was a dark night, the moon had set, and he does not know that stretch of country which is in any case lonely, thinly populated, ill signposted, and traversed by narrow intersecting lanes which do not appear themselves to know which way they are going."

"I should not care to drive about those lanes myself in the dark without a pilot," admitted the Superintendent handsomely. "You have been here longer than I, Vidal, do you know that stretch of country well?"

"Reasonably well, not more than that."

"If you were to ride round on a bicycle, you might pick up something. You know the approximate area where those men went to a farm for petrol. See what you can do."

Vidal knew only the little Campbell had been able to tell him. The farm was north of the crossroads where Campbell had come out upon the main Paris–Orleans road; it was on the lane itself and not approached by a private road, and a hundred yards before or after it—according to which direction one came from—there was a large pasture field with a wide gap in the hedge, not closed by a gate; and beyond this, a strip of woodland.

Vidal was dressed in a tweed jacket, an open-necked shirt, shorts, shoes and socks, and wore no hat; he did not look in the least like a detective sergeant, although his warrant card was in his pocket. He rode fast up the main road until he came to the turning, and thereafter took his way steadily about the convolution of lanes, looking at one farm after another.

Most of them were ruled out by standing back from the road or having no pasture opposite them. He found three which seemed possible enough to call at to ask his way and thereafter to bring the conversation round to disturbances in the night, but without avail.

He came at last to a lane which had, on his right hand, a large area of dry pasture with some mournful-looking cows tethered at wide intervals to iron pegs driven into the ground, round which they nibbled all day, producing an ugly pattern of disconnected circles, like the marks of wet glasses on an ill-kept bar. The field had no gate but a wide-open gap, beyond there was a screen of trees. A hundred yards further on, on his left, there was a farmhouse with outbuildings.

Vidal dismounted when he reached the farm. There was an open space between the house and the road; on either side of this space there were cow sheds, and the middle of the space was occupied by the customary by-products of cow sheds, with its overflow running into the roadside ditch. Vidal, whose nose was no more sensitive than the average Frenchman's, disregarded this and wheeled his bicycle towards the house. As he came up to the open door a man came up the passage inside and stopped on seeing him.

"Good day," began Vidal. "I am extremely sorry to trouble Monsieur, but I have been riding a long time and lost my way. Would it be possible for me to obtain here a glass of milk?"

"I should think so," said the man good-temperedly. "Put up that machine of yours and come into the dairy."

The man was plainly the farmer himself, a heavy-shouldered elderly man, a little bent but having the appearance of immense strength. He filled a pottery mug with milk, gave it to Vidal, and then excused himself for a moment to lean out of the window and shout directions to someone outside about taking something or another to the blacksmith for repair. "Yes, now," he added in reply to a half-audible protest, "we shall be using it tomorrow. Wait, and bring it back."

The dairy was the usual cool, dim, low-ceilinged place with the usual fittings of wide shelves, pails, and setting pans; two or three pairs of yokes hung upon the walls with skimmers and strainers; a butter-churn was upended in a corner.

"My sons," said the farmer, returning the upper half of his person to the dairy, "they think they know more than the old man. Eh? Because they are as tall as I."

Vidal laughed. "Perhaps Monsieur also thought so when he was first full-grown?"

"Perhaps. Perhaps. But I learnt, by degrees, and so will they."

"This is delicious milk," said Vidal.

"Let me refill the mug," said the farmer.

"If you please. Thank you. It must be very quiet here," said Vidal, looking out of the window, "especially in winter."

"We are too busy to trouble whether it is quiet, and for the winter evenings there is always the radio."

"No doubt, no doubt. Tell me, do you ever have trouble with people coming round at night for what they can pick up?"

The farmer's face darkened.

"If we do, monsieur, we can deal with them, I and my sons."

Vidal thought it was time to come out into the open.

"Monsieur, tell me. Did you have any sort of trouble here very early yesterday morning?"

The farmer scowled.

"When? What morning?"

"Today is Friday. Yesterday morning, very early, soon after two o'clock."

"What business is that of yours?"

Vidal set down his mug, took out his warrant card, and showed it to the farmer.

"I am Detective Sergeant Vidal of the Orleans——"

"Then you can get out. I want no police here telling me my business."

"It is my business too. Two men came to this farm to steal petrol, because they had run their tank dry, at about two in the morning of yesterday. They were kidnappers, and their victim was bound and trussed in the car just up the road here. You may have read about it in the paper."

"Haven't read it yet. Evening's when I get a read at the paper."

"A prominent businessman named Dupont."

"For a ransom, I suppose," said the farmer.

Vidal shrugged his shoulders. "In any case, he was released and his rescuer drove the car away. Now, monsieur, I have been frank with you, please tell me your end of the story."

"I did not know," said the farmer slowly, "that they were such serious criminals as that."

"Of course not. How should you?"

"I thought they had come here to steal. The dogs began to bark and we heard what sounded like shots fired, but it might have been a motorcycle backfiring—we had been asleep, and when one is suddenly awakened—— We picked up our shotguns, my sons and I, and came down in our socks and crept out. There was a light in the shed where I keep my car, and the door was open. We jumped in on them and, since they did not desire a charge of shot in the stomach, they came quietly."

"In their place, so should I. Where are they now, do you know?"

"Do I know? Of course I know. Come and see."

Vidal followed the farmer into a sort of back kitchen with a large wooden trap door in the floor.

"Listen," said the farmer.

There was a bumping noise as of someone intermittently kicking something and the sound of a hoarse voice trying to shout.

"They did make more noise at first," said the farmer simply, "but I think their voices be tired."

"But—but—but why didn't you call up the police?"

"Why? We're coming in to market tomorrow. Always come to market Saturdays. We'll bring them in tomorrow."

"But the police would have——"

"Don't want police about here. We'll manage all right. All trussed up with the calf net over them, they won't give trouble. Tomorrow will do for them."

"Have you given them anything to eat?" asked Vidal in almost an awed voice.

"Yes. Oh yes, they've had something to eat."

"Do you think I could look at them? I may be able to recognize them."

"Certainly," said the farmer, and heaved up the flap of the trap door. "If you look down you can see them. There's no danger, they're chained up."

They were, too. When the flap was thrown back there was a rattling of chains and two woebegone, filthy, unshaven faces peered up at them. The cellar was about eight feet deep and the trap was approximately in the middle of it.

"How do you get down there?"

"We put a ladder down when needful. We didn't bother with them; we just lowered them down and let go. They can't lift their arms, so they're quite safe."

Vidal looked down and the prisoners looked up. They were just recognizable if one knew for whom one was looking. Vidal nodded, and the farmer proceeded to close the trap. Immediately there came a hoarse howl from below.

"Let us out, let us out. Food, food, food——"

The farmer shut the trap with a thud.

"Thank you very much," said Vidal tactfully. "You have done a service to the Republic by capturing those two. I will ring up the police and they will bring a van for them. Are you on the telephone, if you please?"

"No, I am not. I don't want them taken away, I want to take them in myself. We captured them, didn't we?"

"Certainly you did, but you——"

"Very well. You ride back to Orleans, young man, and tell the police their prisoners will be along tomorrow."

Vidal fingered his chin. "It will save you two days' keep if we take them away now."

The farmer considered. "That is true, although it is also true that their keep does not cost much."

"You will, naturally, get all the credit."

"And a reward, if there is one?"

"I have not heard that there is," said Vidal with strict if limited truth, "but Monsieur Dupont ought to be grateful."

The farmer stepped back. "There is a telephone in the village half a mile down the road."

When the prisoners had been scraped, scrubbed, provided with clean clothes, and brought before the Superintendent, they looked better but they were much subdued and quite ready to answer questions. The only trouble was that they had so little to say. They had never seen the man who gave them their orders and they had no idea who he was. He was only a voice on the room telephone and they did not know the voice.

By the time Hambledon left the Sûreté offices it was getting late and he decided to stay in Paris that night if only for the satisfaction of hearing, in the morning, who had been buried in the name of Raoul Rougisson, ornithologist. There was little doubt in his mind that it would prove to be Jean Jaboulet, called the Spider; presumably Letord would call in the head clerk of Spiders Anonymous to look at the body.

Hambledon dined in a café in the Rue St. Honoré and thereafter strolled down the Rue Royale to cross the Place de la Concorde and walk beside the Seine under the walls of the Tuileries gardens. May is the month in which to visit Paris. The night was clear and lovely, the moon was almost full, the fountains were playing, and the falling water sparkled in the light from the tall lampposts in the Place de la Concorde; there were strings of electric lights as far as the eye could see along the garden side of the Rue de Rivoli and between the trees of the Champs Élysées until the great bulk of the Arc de Triomphe closed the vista. The Seine's numerous bridges are also, for the most part, outlined with light, and the rippling water below is thick with dancing stars. On the Île de la Cité the sombre magnificence of Notre Dame is floodlit; far away to the north and high in the air, also floodlit, the white mass of the Sacré Coeur hangs in a violet sky.

Hambledon strolled on slowly, content merely to enjoy himself. "If I were a cat," he murmured, "I should purr loudly." Purring not being a human accomplishment, he stopped to light a cigarette, and at that moment one of Letord's detectives passed by, recognized Hambledon, and greeted him in passing.

The spell was broken and Hambledon's thoughts returned to his problem. Power must have had some reason for making a note of the Café de Bruges telephone number; a recent note, too, since the little pad, upon which it was the only entry, was new and clean. If the woman there was not Madame Tiffet she might know her or be able to tell him where she had gone. Or she might have known Power.

Twenty minutes later Hambledon pushed open the swing doors of the Café de Bruges and walked in.

The place was about half full, and the incredibly ancient waiter was tottering about at a surprising speed. The same woman was behind the bar, but there was no one standing there and she was doing a little aimless and ineffectual dusting. Hambledon walked up to the bar, ordered a glass of Beaujolais, and noticed that the lady was red-eyed with a tendency to sniff and not completely and entirely sober. She might even be in a mood to talk.

Hambledon asked her to keep him company in a little glass of something, drank to her health, "A votre santé, madame," and settled down to be a good listener.

"Madame," he began, "seems a little out of spirits tonight. I trust Madame has had no bad news?"

She shook her head mournfully, poured out a glass of colourless liquid which in England would probably have been gin but in that type of place in Paris might have been anything and probably was, and said that Monsieur was most sympathetic as, indeed, anyone could see at first sight of Monsieur. No, she had had no fresh bad news, it was just that today was one of those anniversaries which wring the hearts of women, and hers was being wrung, if Monsieur understood.

Hambledon said that indeed, indeed there were anniversaries in everyone's life which tended to have that effect. Bereavements, he sighed, were the lot of all.

"Mine is no remembered bereavement. No, monsieur, on the contrary. Nine years ago today it was my wedding day."

Hambledon looked across towards the framed licence by the door, and she followed the direction of his glance.

"I was Alphonsine Buchot before I married and came here with my husband. I am of Bruges, monsieur. But after the great scandal I thought it better to go back to my maiden name. No one would wish to be reminded of the name Tiffet."

Hambledon looked blank.

"Monsieur is not of Paris? No, then he will not have heard. One's troubles, when they come, they cover the earth and sky, so we think. La, la, fifty kilometres away no one has heard of them."

"That is always true," said Hambledon. "But Madame's trouble would appear to be out of the common rut." He emptied his glass; she took it from him and refilled it.

"Judge for yourself, monsieur——"

"A cigarette, madame?"

"If you please, yes." He lit it for her and she went on. "I first saw my husband when he came to Bruges and entered for the shooting trophy. Monsieur knows the shooting tournaments of Belgium? Yes. My husband—we were not married then—ah, monsieur, what a shot he was. A hand like a rock and an eye like an eagle's, he won the gold medal, monsieur, think of that. Then, when the shooting was done, my brother brought Julien home, back to the café, for my father kept a café just behind the cathedral. Monsieur knows the cathedral of Bruges, with the belfry? Yes indeed, everyone does. Julien was so handsome. Not big, you understand, but well made, and his face and his hair——" She broke off to blow her nose and sobbed gently.

Hambledon asked himself why on earth he, who hated tears, was listening to this, and there was no answer except that some inner urging told him to persevere. This place, or someone in it, meant something to Power.

"We married, monsieur; we came to Paris and started this café. I had a little *dot*, you understand, and he also had some money, so we were in it as partners. All went very well for a time and we lived, but we could not make money fast enough for him. He was always interested in the Bourse"—the French Stock Exchange—"if he won a little money on a horse or made a deal in fruit or potatoes, it was stocks and shares all the time. Particularly stocks; would this rise or that fall? For me, I do not understand, although Julien spoke continually about them. Monsieur, no doubt, knows all about such things."

Hambledon disclaimed any expert knowledge. "I am no financier as, it seems, your husband was."

"He said that in order to be a financier it was necessary to have a sum of money to deal with." She picked up her empty glass and looked absent-mindedly at it, so Hambledon begged her to refill it at his expense. "Monsieur is most kind. Julien said we should have put our money to dealing in shares instead of in buying this place, but I said that talk was folly, for here at least we have shelter and food. It was soon after that that those men began to come in, and then my good customers would not come and the place began to go down. For, monsieur, quiet decent people will not come to a place which the police are watching. One cannot expect it. I would not, myself."

"Then those men you mentioned were——"

"Criminals, monsieur. Bad types, every one, and he and they used to whisper together in corners. I warned him, but——" She shook her head. "He told me nothing, nothing, but sometimes he had money and it did not come out of the business. Then there came a time when he was at once pleased and a little frightened. I was terrified, but of what I did not know. Then one dreadful night a gang of them came in and sat by the door there grinning evilly together until some sign was given by one outside, and then ah! all in a moment the knives were out and there was a rush this way. I leapt for the stairs there; as I looked back at the turn my husband behind the bar had a gun in his hand and there were shots fired. I rushed upstairs and barred myself in the bedroom; as I did so there were more shots and the big window there broke and fell out. Then there were some yells and then silence, monsieur, silence as of the grave. After a time I could bear it no longer, so I crept out, listening, and down the stairs one step at a time, listening. There was no one there at all, monsieur, neither my husband nor his assailants, and I have never seen him since."

"Dreadful," said Hambledon sympathetically, "dreadful. You assume, then, that he was killed?"

"The police do, monsieur, but, myself, I do not. I agreed with the police in what they said because it was necessary in order to regularize the business, and one must live. For me, I think he got clear away, for while there was blood about the room and upon one of the tables, there was none behind the bar here."

"I see. Is there a back way out from here?"

"Assuredly, monsieur, and half a dozen ways one can go when once one is outside. He knew them all." Madame Tiffet finished her drink, slumped forward with her folded arms upon the bar, and stared fixedly over Hambledon's shoulder. "One of them was hit; there was a mark upon that wall where someone had supported himself with a bloody hand. It was difficult to clean off. Very difficult. One got it clean and then, later, it came back. Faintly, you understand, but visible." Her face changed so abruptly that Hambledon looked round quickly. "It is there now, you see? Beside the little mirror."

Hambledon paid for the drinks and took his leave, but she did not appear to see or hear him. When he was outside in the street he glanced in through the window. The old waiter was taking up Hambledon's money from the bar and putting it in the till, glancing at his mistress from time to time, but she was still leaning motionless upon the counter and staring at a blank space upon the wall.

CHAPTER 15 *Madeleine*

"We were right," said Letord. "The coffin was dug up in the small hours of this morning and by six o'clock the Spider's head clerk had identified the body. Jean Jaboulet in person. I tell you something else. That fingerprint which Monsieur Power had in his wallet, the same as one which we found in Marius Aldebert's apartment after it had been sealed up, after his murder—you remember—that was the Spider's print. Now where are we?"

"Let us clear up as we go," said Hambledon. "It was the Spider at Arnage all that time, calling himself Rougisson, and that accounts for his poking his nose into the Power murder. The Superintendent at Orleans said that the story of Rougisson's doings did not fit Rougisson, and he was perfectly right. It wasn't Rougisson. How the Spider knew that Power's crash was not accidental, I have no idea; he must have seen or heard something. He broke into the mortuary when Power's body was there, to make sure that he was right, and found a bullet wound in the head. All right so far. Two nights later someone climbed into my bedroom window; when he went out of the window again, a shot was fired and the Spider was killed. Was it the Spider in my room or his killer? Stiff beards are regrettably common in France."

"I told you before," said Letord, "that this case is like that; if we do get anything it does not help us. It does not matter in the least whether the man in your room was the Spider or his killer; what does matter is that whereas, before, we were looking for a man with a beard, even that has now been taken from us, for who knows what the man at the bottom of the ladder looked like? I have been discussing this affair with my superiors—superiors in rank, I mean," added Letord with his characteristic twist of the

146

eyebrows, "and we are going to try to crack this nut from the other side. Hitherto these felons commit a crime and we run after them; this time we propose to offer them a crime and see if they commit it. Listen, my friend, do you know anything about Campos de Oro?"

"A small South American republic. Not, I believe, very efficiently organized. I've never been there, if that's what you mean. Why?"

"In spite of being called Fields of Gold," said Letord, translating the Spanish name, "they are in financial difficulties. I suppose they find it difficult to collect their revenues."

"And those that are collected probably don't reach the Treasury," said Hambledon crisply.

Letord lifted his shoulders. "It has been known, and not only in South American republics. Well now, the matter is this. Some years ago a company was formed in Paris to lend money to Campos de Oro on the security of the tramways in Ciudad Aurea —that is the capital. This company toddled along quite well and still does, but it made no one's fortune. You understand, the stock was highly speculative and the dividends paid were not as high as people thought they should be, considering the risk. Still, there were regular dividends, which is more than can sometimes be said for this class of investment."

"I gather they have not had a revolution in Campos de Oro lately."

"My friend, you speak as one having experience of this sort of thing. No, I believe not. Well, now they want some more money, so the company is raising another loan in exchange for control of the country's railways. In effect, Campos de Oro is pawning her transport systems to raise the wind, and the company is offering the public a fresh issue of shares."

"I wonder how old their railway engines are," said Hambledon, "1880 and all that?"

Letord laughed. "It is nothing to me, I am not an investor. The point is this. Two envoys from Campos de Oro are coming to Paris shortly to negotiate about some outstanding details and, if all goes well, to sign. After that the new issue will be placed on the market and the result will be a rise in the value of the old shares as well as of the new ones—they hope, and I daresay they

147

are right. If, on the other hand, the envoys did not sign after all, or only signed after dramatic delays——"

"The bottom would drop out of the Campos de Oro market. Yes, I see where you are leading. If Power's conspirators are not interested in this loan, they are not trying. What are you doing about it?"

"From the moment the envoys disembark at Le Havre they will be watched like your so valuable Crown jewels——"

"Kept in an outsize bird cage and fed through the bars by Beefeaters?"

"I wish we could! Then, at the first faintest sign of any sort of interference, we pounce."

"Splendid. On what?"

"On the interferers. At least," said Letord, looking sideways with raised eyebrows, "that is the official policy, and I have been told to carry it out."

"Umf," said Hambledon, and retired into thought. Letord waited for a long minute and then began ostentatiously to occupy himself with some of the papers on his desk.

"I have been thinking," said Hambledon eventually.

"My felicitations."

"I think this gang will have to do something about this Campos de Oro business. For one thing, it is, as you say, right up their street. For another, Campbell wrecked their Dupont scheme for them only the other day, and their leader will have to do something quickly to take their minds off it. I mean, in organizations like that, prestige is everything to the leader. He's only got to slip twice running and he's finished. Well, he's slipped once. What I was thinking was that it might be a good idea to do something rather more definite than just sit round waiting for them to attack. However, this is your case and I don't wish to butt in——"

"Kindly butt and continue butting——"

"Oh, very well. Do you remember my assistants, Forgan and Campbell? I can't remember whether or not you ever met them personally, but there was an occasion when they posed as a couple of Spanish Communists and addressed a Paris meeting which broke up in disorder——"

"It broke up in a riot," said Letord briskly, "which spread over half a dozen streets, caused thousands of francs' worth of damage,

148

and kept my police running off their feet for a fortnight. Disorder! No, I never met your assistants personally, and if I had met them at that time I should probably have strangled them. Are they still alive? You surprise me."

"They are more than alive, they are at Arnage-sur-Loire. The Campbell who dressed in stripes and rescued Dupont was one of them, Forgan's the other. They spent some years in the Argentine, so that passing as Spanish South Americans is quite simple to them."

"I see, yes. I did not realize that you had two assistants at Arnage and that they were the same two men. Yes, you are going to suggest that they take the place of these two envoys as soon as they land."

"Before they land. My men should go out on the pilot cutter and come ashore as the envoys. You could smuggle the envoys ashore and bring them to Paris, where they can negotiate in privacy and peace. In the meantime, Forgan and Campbell can take whatever comes. If nothing happens, there is no harm done."

"I will put it up to my superiors," said Letord; "it is for them to decide. I shall, in fact, recommend it. There is one thing, my friend. If that gang do try to break into these negotiations and come up against Forganne and Cam-belle, it will not be your men who have to take what comes. It will be the gang. They will have my sympathy. I will even, when it is all over, burn an inexpensive candle over there"—he jerked his head in the general direction of Notre Dame—"for their ultimate benefit. They will need it."

Hambledon returned to Arnage-sur-Loire and told the model-makers to be prepared to impersonate two plenipotentiaries from the Republic of Campos de Oro who were coming to Paris to negotiate a loan. He told the whole story in detail as far as it had gone.

"There is nothing decided yet," he added. "The authorities in Paris have to decide. Again, even if you do take the place of these envoys, nothing at all may happen, in which case you can just fade away."

The two men thought it over for a few minutes.

"May we ask questions?" said Forgan.

"Certainly."

"I suppose," said Campbell, "that it is not their intention to prevent altogether the agreement being signed? They will want to hold things up and set rumours going to discredit the stock until it is so worthless that it's being used to wrap round cabbages at Les Halles. At that point, of course, the gang buys. But after that they will want it signed so as to send up the value of the shares again. I have it right? Same old hookum as the Dupont case?"

"That is the general idea," said Hambledon, "but——"

"But they can't kidnap us," said Forgan. "Those envoys couldn't disappear even for a few days."

"Or the resultant uproar would rock the chancelleries of Europe," said Campbell.

"Hardly that," said Hambledon. "It isn't a government loan and you aren't impersonating the Camposian President."

"Oh, I know. I just like using that phrase," said Campbell. "What we were really wondering was what they were likely to do with us if we've got to be free to visit the company offices and talk turkey about tramways."

"They must be nice to us," said Forgan. "I mean, they can't even toast our toes, can they?"

"I should think they would be perfectly charming to you," said Hambledon. "They will start off, I imagine, by making friends. After that I see three courses open to them; probably there are several more, but three are obvious. One depends on the moral characters of the Camposian envoys. I mean——"

"Blackmail," said Campbell and Forgan with one voice.

"If they have nothing blackmailable in their blameless pasts, the gang could introduce something new. Get you into some really serious trouble in Paris and then twist your tails over that. It has, of course, been done before, and in Paris, too. There was a famous historic example just over a hundred years ago—— However, I digress."

"Tell us all about it some other time, please," said Forgan, "it sounds interesting. But in the meantime, if Campbell and I behave with the most unshakable decorum, what's your third alternative?"

"I think I should have put it first," said Hambledon, "and anyway, you've both thought of it already. A thumping bribe, of course."

"What!" said Campbell in tones of horror. "Bribe a Camposian envoy with a couple of hundred pounds? Inconceivable!"

"Sordid," said Forgan. "And I should think it would be more than that, anyway."

"We have an opportunity of buying the shop next door," said Campbell, "if we had the money."

"I rely implicitly upon you to behave exactly as Camposian envoys might be expected to behave," said Tommy blandly. "Don't count on it, though. Blackmail, if possible, would be cheaper for them."

"So it would. Well now," said Forgan, "since I don't think we can probe any further at the moment into a problematical future, would you like to hear a funny story about a rabbit?"

"I know several, myself," said Tommy, "and at least one of them is in rhyme. What's yours?"

"Some time ago," began Campbell, "we met a small boy who has a tame rabbit; he was gathering fodder for it. It's a chinchilla, one of Barbeau's—he breeds them. He gave this kid this rabbit when it was a kitten or whatever rabbits are when young, because he thought it was going to die, but it didn't. It is part of the plot that this rabbit is a lady. All clear so far? Good. We met our young friend Armand again yesterday, staggering towards his home with a large wooden box from the grocer's. He explained that his rabbit was going to want a larger hutch because she is going to have a family."

"Rabbits are like that," said Hambledon. "Especially female ones."

" 'Does' is the technical term. Yes, they may be, but not if they are the only rabbit in the place except Barbeau's and he—Armand —wouldn't let Barbeau see her because, now she has grown so beautiful, Barbeau wants her back. There are no other rabbits about on account of myxomatosis."

"I see your difficulty."

"So, not believing that rabbits practise parthenogenesis, we questioned the lad further, and it transpired that he had carried Madeleine down to Barbeau's place under his coat and watched his opportunity, when nobody was about, to put her in Barbeau's rabbit run. Now this, Hambledon, was the day when Power was shot."

Hambledon sat up.

"I have your interest, yes?"

"Are you sure it was that day?"

"Armand is. When he eventually got clear away with Madeleine under his coat, he was just putting her back in her hutch when a neighbour's small boy yelled to him to come quick, there'd been a norful car crash and it was on fire and the man was dead all bloody, come and look, so Armand slammed the hutch door shut and rushed off. When he got home again Madeleine had got out because the door wasn't properly latched, hopped into Papa's young lettuces, and mopped up a couple of rows before anybody noticed her. So young Armand got a tanning."

"Please go on."

"Barbeau keeps his chinchillas in a wired-in run behind the hen run. Armand came through the spinney and approached his objective from the back; he had to hang about a bit because old Barbeau was doddering round the yard. He went in at last and Armand emerged from his screen of bushes and dropped Madeleine in among her relations. Then he had to hide again because Monsieur from the hotel—the fair-haired one—came across the yard with a long basket on his arm and went in at the back door of the farm."

"The devil he did!"

"Armand said," put in Forgan, "that he was not surprised to see Monsieur from the hotel go in there, because he knows that Barbeau supplies the hotel with eggs. Go on, Campbell."

"Armand said he was just thinking he'd better wait until Monsieur from the hotel came out again, even if it was rather a long time, because putting a lot of eggs into a basket is a slow business, one has to be so careful, Monsieur understands. However, Monsieur from the hotel was very quick; he came out again almost at once, and Armand thought it must have been a chicken instead of eggs because the basket was not very heavy. What startled Armand was that the manager didn't go back by the path to the hotel, he came through the spinney quite close, and Armand was afraid he'd be seen, but he wasn't."

"Dear me," said Hambledon. "That was a folding gun; one of those long baskets would take it easily. I suppose it's too much to hope that the boy saw what was in the basket?"

Campbell shook his head. "There was a white cloth over it. Besides, I imagine that Armand was flat on his face in the bushes. I have not done, I have more."

"Oh, please," said Hambledon.

"Armand said that he began to wonder whether he ever would get Madeleine out again because old Barbeau came round the corner of the house and kept on pottering about the yard. Time went on and eventually a clock in the farmhouse struck eleven and Barbeau went indoors. Armand waited a few minutes to see if he was coming back and then collected Madeleine and made tracks for home."

"Well, that lets Barbeau out if the story can be substantiated," said Hambledon. "The clock——"

"Maroche says it's a good old clock, a grandfather, and keeps good time; it's never more than five minutes out. Vidal has been checking the story. Armand's father confirms that it was on the day when Power was killed that he walloped his son for letting his rabbit get at the lettuces, and Armand's mama says she saw him come in and go to the hutch at about a quarter or twenty past eleven. It wasn't half-past, she says, because she looked at the clock to see how long it was to dinner when the other boy called Armand out."

"If you came out from Barbeau's back door," said Hambledon, "and walked past the place where the boy was hiding——"

"We went there this morning," said Forgan, "and inspected the geography. You pass the hen run, the rabbit run, and a screen of bushes where Armand was couched like a trembling fawn, and then walk up a steep little meadow which runs up to the crest of a hill. On the top are trees and bushes; penetrate these and you find yourself within a stone's throw of the place where Power was shot. You only have to stroll down the hillside fifty yards and you're there."

"I see. But Lacroix of all people—I mean——"

"I know," said Forgan. "We sympathize."

"We feel for you," said Campbell.

"There's a line of Tennyson's," said Hambledon, "about a 'snowy-banded delicate-handed dilettante priest.' Lacroix isn't a priest so far as I know, but—— Has Vidal interviewed him yet?"

"Even as we sit here talking," said Forgan, "Vidal is applying his corkscrew to the elegant bottle we call Lacroix. He said he would come up here afterwards and tell us the outcome if there is any."

"We talked to our waiter the other day," said Campbell. "By the way, you will be glad to hear that the state of my nerves shows a marked improvement lately, and the waiter no longer plonks down the dishes and bolts out of the room. We discussed with him Barbeau's possible guilt, and he said that the fact that Barbeau's gun was used was, as evidence, completely without value. He says it hangs on the wall in the sort of back-kitchen place one enters to fetch away eggs. He has seen it himself many times when he has been sent down to get the eggs. They are left there on a table, four dozen or five dozen as may be, and one goes down with a basket and just takes them, and very often one sees nobody. Anyone, he says, could watch his chance and take the gun. And put it back again, naturally."

There came a tap at the sitting-room door and Forgan admitted Vidal.

"Any luck?"

"Not much," said the detective with a wry face. "I asked Lacroix whether it was true, as we had been told, that he had been to the Barbeau farm at that time on that day. He said—a little hesitantly, as I thought—that it was. He had half an hour to spare while his tyres were being repaired, so he filled it usefully by going for the eggs. He said he heard and saw no one about at the farm; one often did not. He took his eggs and came away again and that was all. Asked why he had taken another path instead of that by which he came, he said it was because the more direct path was muddy and he was afraid of slipping with his fragile burden— his own words. Asked whether the gun was in its usual place, he said he had not noticed, he took no interest in guns. Well, there you are, messieurs."

"Do you know," said Hambledon, "how many eggs he bought?"

"I asked one of the Barbeau family, the elder son's wife, and she looked it up for me. Four and a half dozen."

"Fifty-four eggs——"

"Which had to be taken out of a large bowl on the table and put in a basket," said Vidal.

"All in the time it took Lacroix to go in and come out again almost at once," said Campbell.

"Carrying a basket which was obviously not heavy," said Forgan.

"Yes, I know," said the detective, "but you could not convict a cat on the evidence of a child of nine giving an estimate of time ten days later."

"In any case," said Hambledon, "much as I would like to, I cannot see Lacroix in the part of First Murderer. Did you get anything else?"

"Only," said Vidal, frowning horribly over a cigarette he was rolling, "only an impression that he was frightened. No, not frightened." He ran the edge of the cigarette paper along his tongue. "Startled. Not that, quite. Put on guard, perhaps." He put the cigarette in his mouth, and Forgan gave him a light. "As though someone had said to him, 'Look out. Danger ahead.' Eh? You know what I mean? He is a silly-looking blighter—no, not silly. What is the matter with me that I cannot find the right words for Lacroix?"

"Letord, in Paris, has already said twice that when we do get anything in this case it takes us nowhere," said Hambledon.

"It is still true," said Vidal gloomily.

"And Barbeau?"

"I shall go into Orleans by the next bus and make my report. I imagine that Barbeau will be released immediately."

"Barbeau," said Campbell, "ought to buy Madeleine a polished mahogany hutch with brass fittings and lined with velvet."

CHAPTER 16 *A Medal for Julien*

THE TRANSATLANTIC LINER from Buenos Aires, Montevideo, Rio de Janeiro, and Pernambuco radioed her arrival off Le Havre and lay to, waiting for the pilot to come aboard, which he did, and several men with him. One in particular found the climb up the pilot's ladder a little difficult, since such things were not in his line; he was in fact the chairman of the Franco-Camposian Company, who had been induced to come because he was known personally to the two envoys. If it is desired to explain to two nervous foreigners that there is probably a plot to kidnap them and thereafter to do what amounts to kidnapping them oneself, confidence must first be established, and the chairman of the F.-C.C. was the man to do it. He did it very well, and the only trouble arose when the Camposian envoys found that they were to be separated from their luggage.

"We understand, señor, and we trust," said Señor Jaime Buonaventure magnificently. "We will go with Your Excellency secretly and live retired, at your word. But our luggage! It contains our beautiful uniforms, our swords, and *all* our underpants."

"Swords?" said the chairman. "I comprehend entirely the señores requiring their pants, but why swords?"

"To add yet greater dignity to these important negotiations," said Señor Manuelo Goyaz, "we have had the honour of being appointed generals in the Army of Campos de Oro. Hence the swords."

"Of course," said the chairman, who had a healthy sense of humour, "of course. Naturally. Obviously. But if these tiresome precautions unfortunately prove to be necessary, I can suggest a solution. I will, señores, myself lend you the uniforms which I myself wore as a fieldmarshal in the glorious Army of the Resistance during the German Occupation. Gold lace, señores, even

156

down the sides of the trousers, and the sword hilts are embellished with turquoises. As for pants, Paris is full of them."

The difficulty having been thus overcome, everything was ready for the landing by the time the liner berthed at the quayside. The gangway was run ashore and passengers came titupping down them; among them, and wearing an air of hauteur mingled with childlike wonder, the two Camposian envoys. One was tall, with red hair, which is uncommon in Campos de Oro but which was due, the envoy would proudly explain, to his having had a Scottish great-grandfather. The other was short, inclining to stoutness, and had dark hair going thin on the crown; his appearance occasioned no surprise at all. They waited on the quayside until their luggage was gathered about them, and then proceeded slowly towards the customs sheds. The luggage had their names and their country of origin painted clearly upon it so that there was no difficulty in identifying them.

They passed customs with the most gratifying ease; the moment they were through the sheds and out on the further side they were greeted with most charming friendliness, mingled with deference, by a group of four men with their hats in their hands and warm shy smiles wreathing their faces. They explained that they were a small but representative group of the Franco-Camposian Company's shareholders who had had the felicity to be chosen by lot to rush down to Le Havre to be the first to greet the envoys of a great and friendly country, united to France by the bonds of culture, purity of motive, and enlightened self-interest. The envoys replied suitably and the whole party drove away together in a hired limousine towards Le Havre railway station. A moment later a gendarme on a motorcycle went off in the same direction.

"They're off," said Hambledon, peering through a dusty window of the customs offices.

"How pleasant it is," said Letord at his elbow, "when one guesses right for once."

The four alleged shareholders and the two alleged envoys travelled together to Paris in perfect amity and a reserved compartment.

"Our company," said one of the shareholders, "has been at pains to reserve for you a suite in one of the best hotels in Paris."

"Thank you," said the dark-haired envoy with a stiff jerky bow.

"This hotel," said the red-haired envoy in a languid voice, "has it indoor sanitation?"

"But," said the shareholder with a slight gasp, "but certainly it has."

"That is well," said the envoy, and looked out of the window.

"The distinguished messieurs will, of course, be the guests of the company during their stay in Paris."

"We have never before visited Paris," said the red-haired envoy with a sudden, brilliant smile. "I trust that the company will understand our desire for a little pleasurable amusement in the intervals of negotiation?"

"It is understood," said the shareholder who appeared to be the spokesman of the party, for the others merely bowed, beamed, and said: "Yes, yes," at appropriate intervals. "It is understood. A program has been tentatively drawn up for your approval. It includes——"

"The Musée du Louvre," said the other envoy.

"Certainly, monsieur——"

"And the Catacombs."

"But certainly. The messieurs are plainly men of the most cultivated tastes."

"We are indeed," said the envoy, and immediately spoiled the effect by winking at the shareholder. There was a general laugh, and the rest of the journey was most enjoyable.

Hambledon and Letord travelled to Paris in a police car which formed the escort to a large limousine that contained the genuine Señores Buonaventure and Goyaz, the genuine chairman of the Franco-Camposian, and a high police official inside, and a much lower police official in plain clothes, but armed, in front beside the chauffeur. The limousine put down its passengers at a small retired house at Issy-les-Moulineaux, a suburb to the south of Paris. The house had a garden surrounded by a high wall, the entrance being closed by iron gates, which were immediately shut and locked after the car had driven in. The garden was pleasant if not very extensive, but there was an air of monastic seclusion about the place, and the señores looked about them a little disconsolately. The chairman noticed it.

"It is only until the negotiations are through and the agreements signed," he said encouragingly. "Then, when all is done and our consciences are clear, we will show the señores our Paris, yes? Duty first, of course, but pleasure afterwards, *hein?*"

The señores cheered up visibly.

Life in Paris settled down while Hambledon and Letord waited patiently for what should come. Forgan and Campbell attended punctually at the F.-C.C. offices for the first two days; after that their enthusiasm waned sensibly and they took to arriving soon after eleven, which gave them time for a chat with Hambledon and a cigarette or so before they went out to lunch at twelve. The French do not hurry over meals nor expect their visitors to do so; lunch lasted until two o'clock, when Forgan and Campbell returned, with furrowed brows and the preoccupied air of the important business executive, to the company's offices until four, when they broke off for the day.

In the meantime the real negotiations were being conducted behind high walls, guarded by police, in the villa at Issy-les-Moulineaux. The company's high executives travelled there every day, the Señores Buonaventure and Goyaz did not leave the grounds, and the secret was well kept. The señores may have become bored in the intervals of business, but at least they were unmolested.

"I believe we give satisfaction," said Forgan on the third day. "We have, of course, been asked how long these negotiations are likely to take. Have you any idea?"

Hambledon shrugged his shoulders. "I'm told that they should be over inside a week, but one can't tell. If they strike a snag and both sides turn obstinate, one never knows. Does it make it awkward for you, hanging on indefinitely?"

"On the contrary," said Campbell with a wide grin.

"Completely so," said Forgan. "We are being implored and, I may say, induced——"

"By the payment of an adequate—or nearly adequate—sum, which we have insisted upon receiving in advance——"

"To hold up the signing for as long as possible. We are asked to give as long notice as possible of the date of the signing; that is why I asked you."

"In order that rumours may have time to get round that there may not be agreement after all. It is naturally desired to buy these shares when the price has reached the final depths of despair," said Campbell.

"We have, of course, no control at all over the date when the agreements are signed," said Hambledon. "This is a genuine business deal and we can't interfere. But we can hold up publication of the news for a couple of days if that will help you."

"It might, yes. We'll let you know," said Forgan. "In the meantime, we are going to earn our—our friends' gratitude, shall I say, by being most assiduous in the business."

"In the meantime," added Campbell, "we are their guests and they take us out in the evenings. I must say the Tour d'Argent puts on a perfectly edible dinner."

"And the Folies Bergères a very likable show," said Forgan. "I'm only sorry the Bal Tabarin isn't running at the moment."

"Dear me," said Hambledon, "do you mean to tell me that they stand for that sort of thing? You'll eat up all the profits at that rate."

"If they hesitate, we have only to turn ponderous and say how little, now, remains between the high contracting parties and complete agreement——"

"And they stand us an evening out at Le Boeuf sur le Toit. I say," said Campbell, "they must be going to make a killing."

"Are they still the same four who met you at Le Havre?"

"Still the same, though not always all at once. Does Letord know anything about them?"

"Quite a lot," said Hambledon. "Tell me, no one of the four is the real kingpin, is he?"

"Oh no. If we make any suggestion, they say that they will consider it. An hour or two later we get the answer. Consultations with somebody?"

"I imagine so. By telephone, probably."

Hambledon was a little at a loose end. He dared not leave Paris in case the expected crisis should arise the moment his back was turned, and equally he dared not take any effective measures against the conspirators for fear of setting off the explosion prematurely. Letord was having the four "shareholders" watched and their contacts noted, but so far the watch had produced no information that was worth the trouble.

It occurred to Tommy Hambledon that he had still not found out what there was about the Café de Bruges which had induced

Power to note its telephone number. It might, of course, have been something merely temporary; someone staying there for a few days, for example. Perhaps Power had, himself. One could at least ask whether they ever took in lodgers. Lodger, he felt, was the right word to use for anyone staying at the Café de Bruges; it was definitely below the social strata which takes in "guests."

He went there one morning; when he pushed open the swing doors Madame, behind the bar, looked up and seemed pleased to see him. She was certainly looking better than she had the last time he was there; her flowered overall was clean and her hair was tidily arranged.

"Ah, monsieur! I am glad to see Monsieur here again."

Hambledon replied suitably and, when the formality of ordering drinks was over, offered her a cigarette and entered into conversation.

"I am very glad," he said, "to see Madame in better spirits this morning."

"Indeed, monsieur, I am myself again today. I am very angry with myself for letting Monsieur see me as I was the other night. What an exhibition! Deplorable!"

"But madame was naturally distressed——"

"A woman of self-respect should control herself better. What Monsieur could have thought of me!"

"Only that I had come in at an unhappy moment." Hambledon turned and looked down the room; even that seemed brighter and cleaner, and the ancient waiter, still dashing about on spindly legs, appeared to be merely hurried and not harassed. The customers were chattering animatedly together, and even the floor had been thoroughly scrubbed.

"Madame has, no doubt, a nice business here."

She lifted her shoulders and pursed her lips.

"Not so good as it might be if there was a man in the place."

"Your waiter——"

"Ah! I meant, in authority. To help me organize it. My sister helps me in the kitchen, but she is shy, she will not appear. When her husband was drowned—he was a fisherman—she came to me. She is very kind and very useful, but not like a man of one's own."

"No. No, of course not."

"The business could be made to be very good. I have been remiss, I have not had the ambition. So long as there was enough to keep us going, I have not troubled. But, with an incentive, much more could be done."

"No doubt. I have sometimes wondered," said Hambledon casually, "whether Madame ever took in lodgers. The house seems large for two ladies alone."

Her face lit up. "I have not done so, hitherto—— Let me refill Monsieur's glass. But there is no reason why I should not; as Monsieur says, there are rooms enough. There will be, of course, redecoration necessary; I have been neglectful, I admit it. But the house is sound and it is my own."

"I felicitate Madame."

"Tomorrow I go round the house and see what needs to be done and obtain estimates for the work. I would not like Monsieur to see it as it is now, but in a week or two weeks' time, ah, then it will be different. Monsieur is staying in Paris?"

"I may be here for some time," said Hambledon, wondering whether it would be wise to show her Power's photograph and ask whether she had ever seen that man. On second thoughts, better not. If she did know Power, the word might go round that here was someone interested in him and this someone had worked back as far as the Café de Bruges. If she did not know him, no useful purpose would be served.

She pulled open a drawer and took an envelope from it. "Look, monsieur," she said with a laugh which was positively coquettish, "I was not always the sad-faced misery whom Monsieur first met. This is a photograph of my husband and myself on our wedding day. It is true that I was younger then, but happiness is all, is it not?"

Hambledon took the photograph, glanced at it with perfunctory politeness, and then nearly dropped it. The stout young woman could have been Madame and doubtless was, but the husband! That oddly round head of shining fair hair, the small, neat features, the nose slightly turned up, the lower lip pouting, the trim figure which would almost certainly become rounded with advancing years. Lacroix, the manager of the Hotel de la Poste, the man who was frightened of firearms, who turned faint at the sight of blood——

It occurred to him that it was just possible for her to have given him the wrong photograph by mistake.

162

"This is indeed yourself?"

"Myself, monsieur!"

"It is true, at a second glance one sees, but it does not do you justice, madame. So that is your husband?"

"That is he. On the left side of his coat, there, that medal, you see? It is the gold medal he won for shooting, as I told you."

Of course, it would be. And the man who killed Power was a good shot and could handle firearms. Hambledon's face took on momentarily such a grim expression that Madame may be pardoned for jumping to a mistaken conclusion.

"Listen, monsieur. I am now convinced that I have been wrong all these last three years in thinking him still alive. I am sure now that he was killed here that night and will never come back to trouble me. I am free!"

Hambledon was only attending to her with about one tenth of his mind, which was mainly otherwise occupied. To get on to Letord at once, or, failing him, the Superintendent at Orleans. This——

"So," said Madame with a girlish titter, "Monsieur sees that he has no need to be jealous!"

A great light burst upon Hambledon and appeared to swirl round him in loops of coloured fire. Of course she would think that, with him hanging about for no obvious reason, asking her if she ever let rooms—golly!

He handed back the photograph. "I was thinking, madame, how sad it was. So young, so *gentil*, showing such promise, and then to slide into so dreadful an abyss. It is a tragedy that you have lived through."

She drew back, steadied and serious at once. "Monsieur is right," she said, putting the photograph away. "It was indeed a tragedy."

Hambledon talked for a few minutes longer, finished his cognac, and took his leave gravely, as one saddened by the ironies of fate. The moment he was out of sight of the window he took his hat off and wiped his brow.

"Thank Heaven," he said to himself, "I need not go there again; that bit of job's done. If anyone has to, let it be Campbell. Phew! Now, where's the nearest telephone?"

CHAPTER 17 *One Happy Man*

HAMBLEDON rang up Letord's office at the Prefecture; yes, Letord was there; yes, he would be very glad to see Hambledon, especially if, as appeared from his tone, he had something exciting to tell. Tommy hurried off to the Quai des Orfèvres.

"Letord, I think I know who the leader of this gang may be. Probably is. Julien Tiffet, formerly of the Café de Bruges, missing, believed dead; now the manager of the Hotel de la Poste at Arnage-sur-Loire, calling himself Pierre Lacroix."

"What, that man? I understood you to say that he was a shy retiring little man who fainted at the thought of bloodshed and——"

"I know I did. I was wrong, that's all. Madame Tiffet showed me his photograph, and there is no possible mistake. He is a crack shot; he won the gold medal in a shooting tournament at Bruges. He was always playing the stock markets; to her knowledge he was doing that nine years ago. He was always thinking up schemes for getting rich quickly. He ran a gang here in Paris which was at least sometimes successful because, as she says, he often had money that did not come out of the business. In the end he quarrelled with his gang—probably cheated them—and about six of them went down to the Café de Bruges one night to settle their account with knives. He settled it for them with a gun and got clear away. Now look at Arnage. Someone there shot Power and the Spider and was playing the stock markets with the help of a gang for the strong-arm side of the business. Well?"

"Very well indeed," said Letord, picking up his telephone receiver. "Get me the Superintendent of Police at Orleans, please. Yes, in person. Thank you." He replaced the receiver. "What put you onto this, just that telephone number? Nothing more? You do hang on, do you not? I remember years ago describing your arguments as the British bulldog in the act of not letting go. How many times did you go to that Café de Bruges before you got this? Three times, and always it might have been the number for someone staying there a few days only——"

"I thought of that, but she does not take in lodgers. No, not only that. You know, Letord, as well as I, that persistent feeling that there is, after all, something there if one tries just once more? Of course you do. In England we call it a hunch."

"I do, of course, but if it involved repeated visits to a widow—she cannot be so old—I think I should not listen. What? Do I see you in the grip of embarrassment? Tell me, what persuasions did you use to see that photograph? I can see you——"

The telephone bell rang, considerably to Hambledon's relief, for Letord upon the subject of women was apt to be a trifle French.

Letord spoke to the Superintendent at Orleans and gave him a rapid outline of what Hambledon had discovered and of Lacroix's previous history. "It is no part of my duty to give you any orders, Monsieur le Surintendant, but I know what I should do in your place!"

"So do I," said the Superintendent joyfully, "and it shall be done at once."

Detective Sergeant Vidal was at Arnage that morning, engaged in the wearisome task of trying to establish a detailed timetable of Lacroix's movements on the morning when Power was killed, by questioning people who (a) could not remember having seen Lacroix, (b) remembered seeing him that day but not at what time, and (c) remembered his passing the house just after eleven by the clock, but as it had stopped overnight there was a little difficulty, Monsieur understood. Yes, yes, the clock said seven minutes past eleven until it was mended two days later. Yes, yes, but Monsieur understands that one glances at a clock from habit. . . .

Vidal was just telling himself that if there was much more of this sort of thing he would resign from the police and join the Navy, when he saw at a distance Constable Maroche come out of the police cottage, look up and down the street and, on seeing Vidal, advance to meet him with long strides. Wanted on the telephone, *mon sergent*, urgently, by Monsieur le Surintendant at

Orleans. Yes, himself in person. No, he did not say what it was about.

Vidal dashed to the telephone and was told to take Maroche with him to the Hotel de la Poste and there detain for questioning one Pierre Lacroix, so called, although it seemed that it was not his real name and that he was a criminal and the associate of criminals.

"What?" gasped Vidal. "That pink-nosed rabbit?"

"Probably our murderer," said the Superintendent coldly. "Let there be no msitake, Vidal."

Vidal set down the telephone receiver and told Maroche the news.

"If it had been anyone but our Superintendent, and you can't mistake his voice," said Vidal, "I would have said that one played a joke on us."

"There is," said Maroche, buckling his forty-six-inch belt, "after all, a good deal of evidence pointing to Lacroix."

"Yes, I know, but——" said Vidal, and left the sentence unfinished.

When they reached the gravel sweep where cars turned round at the front door of the Hotel de la Poste, Lacroix was out there himself, making encouraging statements about lunch to a party of three who had just arrived in a sports car. Two ladies had already alighted; the driver was still in his seat preparing to back the car into a patch of shade. The two policemen walked straight up to the group.

"Monsieur Lacroix," said Vidal in an official voice, "a moment of your attention, please."

The peremptory tone was unmistakable. The ladies drew nervously together; the driver hesitated and reopened his door. Lacroix looked hard at the police for a second, and his face was neither kindly nor irresolute. The next moment he leapt into the car on the passenger's side, thrust the driver out of his way—he fell out on his head on the gravel—slipped into the driver's seat, and drove furiously away; if Maroche had not leapt for his life he would have been killed. There was a squeal of tyres as the car turned out of the drive into the main road, a diminishing whine from the engine, and that was all.

Vidal had leapt at the car but had become entangled in the flailing legs and arms of its naturally indignant driver. The detective sergeant tore himself loose, rushed into the hotel, and threw himself on the telephone. Lacroix had escaped in a stolen car of such a make, number so-and-so, heading towards Orleans from Arnage; a fast car, yes, but of a conspicuous peacock-blue colour——

He had to wait while his Superintendent sent out orders in all directions for the car to be traced and stopped; he had to wait again, and in silence, while his Superintendent, who was disappointed, humiliated, exasperated—in a word, boiling with fury— addressed to him such winged words as a turmoil of seething emotions suggested. Finally Vidal was told to go through Lacroix's private rooms at the hotel and pack up every single thing that had been his. The search, added the Superintendent, would be efficiently carried out, and a police car would be sent out from Orleans to carry home the harvest. Since Lacroix had left in such a hurry there might conceivably be something, but if Vidal overlooked so much as a used postage stamp he would find himself in uniform again, directing the Orleans traffic on market days for the miserable remainder of his service career. Garrrh!

Vidal replaced the receiver, sighed deeply, and desired the undermanager to conduct him to Lacroix rooms. Lacroix, he added, was being sought by the police on a number of serious charges and had temporarily evaded arrest. Gallet, the undermanager, it may be remembered, could not stand Lacroix at any price, and his unfeigned delight at the news was such as to go some way towards comforting Vidal. In one's worst moments it is pleasant to see someone else completely happy.

Vidal's discoveries included a notebook full of rather cryptic entries, a really large sum of money hidden away under the floorboards, a nine-millimetre revolver which subsequenty proved to be that used to shoot the Spider outside Hambledon's bedroom window, and a chequebook.

The car was not found until the following morning, for it had been driven into the depths of a wood and left there. Only a little over two kilometres away there was a branch-line railway station where the staff vaguely remembered having issued a ticket to

Paris to a tubby little man they did not know by sight. The hunt, accordingly, was shifted to Paris.

"You know," said Letord, "I could almost begin to be sorry for Lacroix."

"The man who shot Power," said Hambledon grimly. "Power was a friend of mine. Personally, I will begin to be sorry for Lacroix when he is dead."

"I am tactless," said Letord instantly. "I am a blundering fool with two left feet and I put them both in my mouth every time I open it. Please forgive me. I was really admiring the truth of the remark in Holy Writ that the way of transgressors is hard."

"If I had my way, Lacroix's would be paved with red-hot hobnails. But what has induced you to these pious reflections?"

"I have already told you how Lacroix fled from the hotel at Arnage at a moment's notice. My friend, he did not even take his hat. I have just learned what the Orleans police found in his rooms when they searched. Over seven million francs and a chequebook."

"The seven million francs, presumably, being to buy Franco-Camposian shares when they had dropped far enough. And the chequebook?"

"A Paris bank. We rang them up, giving them the numbers of the cheques, and they told us that the depositor was a certain Marcel something, I forget. But the point, my friend, is that the poor Monsieur Lacroix must be damned hard up. Eh? So the officials at that bank are awaiting the arrival of Monsieur Marcel who-knows-who when he comes in to sing a sad little song all about how he has lost his chequebook and may he have another one, please, as he wishes to make a withdrawal?"

"Whereupon they will all say, 'But certainly, monsieur, pray take a seat for a moment while we cancel entries and make others——' "

"And ring up my police," said Letord cosily.

At Issy-les-Moulineaux the agreement was eventually signed, but the news was withheld from the public at the request of the Sûreté.

Lacroix, if he was in Paris, as seemed most probable, had gone to ground somewhere, and no amount of watching Forgan's and

Campbell's kindly hosts had uncovered a hint of his whereabouts. Forgan and Campbell had fallen into a routine of sleeping every afternoon at the Franco-Camposian Company's offices in order to be fresh and rested for the night's entertainment. At night they turned out full of sparkle and general *joie de vivre*, all ready to hit it up in the night life of Paris until about five in the morning, while their escorts, although there were four of them, were going over at the knees with the strain of keeping up. For one thing, the alleged Camposian envoys liked walking, especially at night, and Paris is a large city. "Taxi? Oh no, my dear fellows, why? Consider that we cannot bear the thought of wasting the money with which you are already so generous. Besides, walking is a healthful exercise and we must consider our figures, must we not? Let us stroll up again to Montmartre." And since the pseudo envoys' idea of a stroll was a steady heel-and-toe four-and-a-half miles an hour, and since Montmartre is on the top of what is practically a cliff four hundred feet high, one cannot but sympathize with the unhappy crooks.

Nor was this the end of their troubles, for they were running short of money. Anxiety made them careless, so that Forgan and Campbell managed to overhear a conversation through a door which was not quite shut.

"Beppi," said one, "tell me. What the hell has happened to our *patron?*"

"I do not know," said Beppi in a worried voice. "Twice, as you know, Pierre, I have gone to ask if there is a telephone message, but no."

"We are running short of money," said Pierre, snapping his fingers.

"You are mistaken, we have already run out. Le Poisson had to pay for that little party at the Caveau de la Terreur last night and that——"

"I know. He told me, several times. How long is this to go on, Beppi? Those shares are low, but they should go lower."

"*Le patron* said that he would see to rumours being set off, but I have heard no hint."

"It will not matter soon how low they go," said Pierre with an angry laugh. "Very soon, at this rate, they will be too dear for us at five francs each."

"*Le patron* said that he would pass the word when to buy, and no doubt he will also provide the money. Take courage, Pierre. We have done very well with him this three years, have we not? This is to be our big *affaire*; when it is over we can all retire to the country and live honestly. No doubt there is some temporary hitch and he is dealing with it."

"I hope so," said Pierre in a doubtful voice. "I wish now we had not paid those lousy Camposians so much all at once; we could do with it now. Half down and half when it is all over would have been better; I said so at the time."

"They have done their part faithfully, these Camposians, you must admit that. The tall one with a Scotch grandmother asked me last night for how many more days we wanted the signing held up. I did not know what answer to make, not having heard from *le patron*. I said another two or three days at least. He said they would soon be running out of excuses for delay, that if it went on one of them must retire to bed with *la grippe*."

"I wish to heaven they would, then at least they would not walk!"

Hambledon was like a cat on hot bricks these last few days. It seemed to him that no one was doing anything when there was so much to be done, though his common sense told him severely that to spring the trap prematurely was the surest way of not catching his mouse. He wandered about Paris with an ill-defined hope of happening to see Lacroix, formerly Tiffet. Since Lacroix had had no grounds for suspicion of Hambledon, the sight of him would give no cause for alarm, and Tommy drew for himself charming mental pictures of encountering Lacroix casually in some street, greeting him with perfectly genuine enthusiasm, and steering him by the elbow into the warm embrace of the nearest gendarme. However, like most pipe dreams, this one did not materialize.

Hambledon, finding himself one evening near the Île de la Cité, turned into the Préfecture for a word with Letord. There might be some news. There was.

He was in the act of entering that doorway in the great court-yard which led to Letord's office, when he met one of Letord's staff coming out. The man recognized Hambledon and stopped.

"Monsieur is going to visit Monsieur le Chef?"

"I thought of doing so. Is he not there?"

"Oh yes, he is there." The man laughed wryly. "Is Monsieur by any chance wearing an asbestos waistcoat?"

"Shall I need one? What has happened?"

"Monsieur le Chef will tell Monsieur."

Hambledon went inside and was taken to Letord's room by a police clerk with a preternaturally solemn expression. The moment Tommy walked into the room Letord looked up and uttered a stream of comments which were best represented by a mixture of asterisks and exclamation marks.

"Dear me," said Hambledon. "Shall I retire until you are calmer?"

"Calmer," said Letord, and went on with what he had been saying. "That fellow," he added more coherently, "has done it again."

Hambledon sat down and lit a cigarette.

"I assume that you refer to Lacroix."

"You are right. I do. He went to the bank which had issued that chequebook we found and told a perfectly plausible story to account for his having lost it, just as we supposed he would. They did exactly as we had told them to do; they asked him to sit down while they looked up the book in question in order to stop the cheques in case of unauthorized usage, asked him how many cheques he had used out of it, and so on, all the time waiting for one of my policemen to come in. All this—it was just before closing time and the bank was empty of customers—all this went off so well until the door opened and my man walked in."

"In uniform?" asked Hambledon.

"You would ask that. Yes. My man looked at Lacroix and walked towards him. Lacroix got up from his chair, shot my man in the shoulder, dodged round his falling body, and went out of the door before anybody could do anything. I mean, those clerks——"

"Are behind not only a barricade but also a stout brass grille."

"Yes. Yes. I suppose I am unreasonable. When someone eventually did get round to look out of the door, of course he was out of sight. He was probably three streets away. He was probably window-shopping in the Rue de Rivoli. He was probably sitting

at a table in the Place du Tertre drinking a glass of wine. He
was——"

"Cheer up," said Hambledon.

"Cheer——"

"He still hasn't got any money," said Tommy Hambledon.
"Have you put a man on to watch the Café de Bruges?"

CHAPTER 18 *Shareholders' Meeting*

WHILE all this was happening there was another body of people who were rapidly becoming exasperated over the apparent delay in signing the agreement; the genuine shareholders. They were rightly expecting the value of their shares to go up when the good news was told; they wanted to sell out on the top of the rise and make a little honest money for themselves. The days passed, no announcement was made, and misgivings seized upon them. The French are not a people to sit down quietly under circumstances like these; if they are annoyed they say so. A few of them consulted together, notified as many more as they could find to hand, and arranged a demonstration.

Campbell and Forgan awoke happily from their afternoon's rest and went down to the entrance of the Franco-Camposian's marble halls to be unexpectedly faced with a quite sizable crowd in the street outside. The crowd were not yet noisy but they were milling uneasily about, and every now and again a group would start a sort of chant of "Sign! Sign! Sign!" Then the chant would die down again and the crowd waited.

"Now what?" said Forgan.

"Is there, perhaps," said Campbell, "a back door to these baronial halls?"

But at that moment all four men of their escort skipped up the three marble steps and appeared at their elbows. They looked a great deal less amiable than usual and a great deal more efficient; in fact, tough. Two of them attached themselves to Forgan and two to Campbell, and at that moment the crowd noticed the Camposian envoys standing at the head of the steps and looking down on them. The envoys had their heads slightly to one side and wore expressions of shy friendliness.

Immediately a cry went up. "It is they! The Camposians!" for their photographs had been taken at Le Havre and had appeared in the papers. "*Signez, signez!*"

"There's going to be trouble," said Beppi in a low tone. "Get across the road to that café. Push your way through, we will take care of you."

Forgan and Campbell drew themselves up, took off their hats and bowed, smiling widely, to the crowd. Then they replaced their hats, walked unconcernedly down the steps with their escort closely round them, and pushed their way through the crowd. Whenever the press became hamperingly close, they again took off their hats and beamed upon the persons nearest to them, who instinctively fell back to let them pass. They reached the café and passed in through the large glass door which Pierre shut and bolted behind them. The escort drew long breaths of relief.

"That was good," said Beppi approvingly, and patted Forgan on the shoulder. "You did that very well."

"Oh, my dear friend," said Forgan deprecatingly, "these little disturbances, what are they? Presently the soldiers come with guns and shoot the rioters, the rest run away, and then we all go home, no?"

"In your country———" began Pierre, hesitated and started again. "In your country they call out the soldiers, do they, for— for——" He waved his hand towards the crowd.

"Oh yes," said Forgan amiably, "every time. Our people are not very highly civilized, you know. Not always good. But our army is magnificent. We ourselves are honorary generals, did we tell you?"

The café was empty except for one man sitting alone at a table at the back of the room, hardly discernible in the shadows.

"Order coffee, Pierre," said Beppi. "This may blow over; if not, I expect there is a way out at the back."

Pierre beckoned to the waiter and gave the order, and the six men sat down at a table in the middle of the room. Someone tried the door handle and then, when the door did not open, shook it and rattled the handle. Faces could be seen pressed against the glass door, menacing fists were shaken, and confused cries of "Come out!" "Let's us in!" "Sign, sign!" could be heard.

"Shareholders, I suppose," said another of the escort.

"More shareholders, you mean," said Campbell with a semicircular bow to include the company present.

"They recognized you," said Beppi.

"Our poor faces," said Forgan, "have been most efficiently publicized."

The waiter came back with the coffee just as people began banging on the glass panel of the door. He set the tray down hurriedly and ran away to the back of the café, calling, "Monsieur! Monsieur!" A tall man, who was evidently the proprietor, emerged from a doorway, regarded the scene outside with horror, and disappeared again, followed by the waiter.

"It is all right," said Campbell. "He has gone to ring up the commander-in-chief. It is always done like that."

The proprietor returned, carrying a long bottle which he brandished by the neck like a club. He was followed by the waiter, who was armed with one of those heavy wooden mallets which are used for doing whatever is necessary to barrels of alcoholic content. Even as they walked smartly through the café towards the door, someone picked up one of the heavy café chairs upon the *terrasse* outside and drove it through the glass panel of the door, and immediately the angry hubbub of the crowd flowed in like a tide. The glass fell in bodily, and the man who had broken it began to climb in through the hole.

The waiter leapt towards him and dealt him a swinging forehand blow with the mallet on the top of his head; the intruder fell back through the door and rolled upon the ground outside.

"A good stroke, Buonaventure," said Campbell, addressing Forgan. "One would say, a tennis player of merit."

"You are right, Goyaz," answered Forgan. "A champion, by rights. But what is this that now we see?"

The crowd seemed to have lost interest in the café for the moment and to be pushing and milling sideways as though some sort of pressure were being applied along the street. A banner came into view, outstretched high above men's heads upon two poles borne by stalwarts, a homemade banner consisting of a long white strip with letters roughly painted on it. "Down with Taxes," it said, and staggered forward to be joined by another demanding "No More Taxes." "Long Live Poujade" followed and, close upon his heels, "Justice for the Small Shopkeeper."

175

Pierre laughed suddenly. "It is, of all things, a Poujadist procession," he said.

The procession tried to push through and the crowd closed up, there was some laughter and some booing, one of the banners wavered and sank like an expiring flame.

"If they will kindly amuse each other till the police come," said Beppi, "we may yet——"

There was a sudden roar from the crowd, and all the movement ceased. The roar grew louder and high-pitched yells rang out. "Hang them!" "Sign, sign!" There were countercries of "No violence! Order!" and even, believe it or not, "Police!"

"Look," said Pierre, and pointed a long forefinger. "On the steps."

There were four dignified figures in the Franco-Camposian entrance at the top of the steps; four men in top hats, frock coats, and striped trousers, with gold watch chains across pale lavender or buff waistcoats.

"The directors," said Forgan with a gasp, and Beppi turned sharply.

"Is that who they are?"

"It is indeed, and I think that in their place I should have stayed indoors."

"Sign!" yelled the crowd. "Sign the agreement. Sign!"

One of the directors stepped forward and held up his hand, and silence fell.

"My friends! You must trust us. All is well."

"Have you signed—have you—have you signed——"

"My friends——"

There was an ugly rush up the steps, and the directors were swept down into the crowd. A top hat flew up into the air.

"Listen, you fools," yelled one of them in a voice like a bull, "the agreement is signed already. IS SIGNED. Four days ago."

Beppi turned upon Forgan and Campbell. "Signed four days ago? Is that true?"

"Certainly not," said Forgan. "He is but lying to get himself out of trouble with this crowd."

"We have signed nothing whatever," said Campbell in the ringing accents of perfect truth. "But I think we had better sign tomorrow, whatever your *patron* has to say. Eh, Buonaventure?"

"Certainly, Goyaz," answered Forgan. "If this company makes itself too bad a smell, no one will want the shares after all."

"They will say, a swindle," said Campbell, throwing out his arms in a despairing gesture, and there was a horrified silence in the café.

Not so outside. Some of the crowd were in favour of the directors being given another chance; some even believed that the agreement had been signed, in which, of course, they were perfectly right. Others, the majority, were in favour of throwing these directors into the discard and appointing fresh ones. To make their point clear, they proceeded to throw the directors. By the time these unfortunate gentlemen had been rescued and re-captured several times they presented a markedly shop-soiled appearance inconsistent with dignity.

There were, a little further along the street, three large limousines waiting to take the directors home. The cars were, of course, facing towards the trouble. The chauffeurs realized that it was their duty to extricate their masters; they got out of their cars and dived into the mob with that intention. Only one of them, a particularly bright young man, had the intelligent idea of turning his car round before leaving it; facing the other way, it would be ready to drive off. He was the last in the line; he backed away, turned in the road, and then got out. Armed with a tyre lever, he advanced into battle.

Marcel Bourjois was an elderly barrow-boy who dealt in fruit. That morning he had acquired a quantity of melons at a very favourable price indeed because they were all quite ripe and some of them excessively so. The French housewife is no fool. He sold all those which were merely ripe and was left with a load of excessively-so's rapidly getting worse. Melons are heavy and the day was hot. He was a little deaf and also preoccupied; he did not notice the tumult until he rounded a corner into it. He was muttering to himself that if only somebody would take them off him he would—almost—give the condemned things away.

His wish was immediately granted, for melons make excellent missiles, and the squashier they are, the more effective. They were an excellent riposte to the prodding poles of the Poujadists.

Within the café Beppi brooded for a time and then made up his mind.

"You, messieurs," he said to Forgan and Campbell, "will please to make your way out through the back here." A Poujadist pole came through the broken window and the proprietor had to leap to avoid it. "You see? But have no fear. We will guard your rear and join you outside. At once, please."

The Englishmen agreed. In any case, the advice was sensible, for the party in the street was getting rough. They got up and walked together towards the back of the café, where the solitary man still sat at his little table and looked towards them as they came. As soon as they were near enough to see him plainly——

"Do you see what I see?" said Campbell in a rapid mutter in English.

"Face it out," said Forgan in the same tone. "We may get away with it."

When they reached the table the man stood up and confronted them. They looked at him casually for a second, and then the light of recognition dawned on their faces.

"Ah, Lacroix!" said Forgan in a kindly tone. "Having a little jaunt to Paris, eh? You have not chosen a very quiet day for it, have you?"

"Naughty men outside," said Campbell, "very naughty. We think we go home."

"Stop, please," said Lacroix. "Who are those men with you?"

"Just casual acquaintances at our table," said Forgan. "Like ships that pass in the night—you know the hackneyed quotation."

"Nonsense," said Lacroix sharply, "you came in with them. Who are they, please?"

"Friends of ours," said Forgan coldly, "and no business of yours, Lacroix."

"Your friends are my business," began Lacroix, but the four men of the escort, seeing that their charges were being held up, came to see what was happening.

"I thought I told you to get away," said Beppi.

Lacroix moved forward and addressed Beppi. "Who are these two men?"

Beppi asked him what the this-and-that it had to do with him. Who was he, anyway? The careful pretence of manners, which had draped like dust sheets the uncouth outlines of the escort, was slipping off faster with every passing moment.

Lacroix put his hand in his pocket and brought out a tiny cardboard box such as jewellers use for packing small articles. He opened it and turned out the contents upon the table. Three dried beans, cream-coloured with brown markings. The escort stared at them; the Englishmen merely glanced at them with a plain lack of interest.

"Does that mean that he is *le patron?*" asked the most taciturn of the escort; a man who spoke so seldom that, when he did, his associates were always surprised. He took a matchbox from his coat and slid out the contents into his palm, looking from one set of beans to the other. "That is right," he nodded, "it is *le patron*." He smiled and gave the sort of shapeless salute which porters give when they have been tipped.

"Of course!" cried Beppi. "Monsieur, I have been waiting for days to hear from you. Have you——"

"Who are these men?" persisted Lacroix with a jerk of his head towards Campbell and Forgan, now modestly in the background.

"These gentlemen," said Beppi cheerfully, for he seemed to think that his anxieties were at an end, "these amiable gentlemen are the accredited envoys of Campos de Oro who have come to . . ."

His voice tailed off to silence, for Lacroix looked as though he would burst with fury; he was so angry that he stammered.

"You—you—you drivelling half-wits! They are not, they——"

"But they are!" shouted Beppi. "We met them coming off the boat; they had their luggage, their passports, their——"

Lacroix mastered himself with an effort. "Try to take this in," he said. "They were staying at Arnage-sur-Loire for three weeks before ever the Camposians reached Le Havre. Got that? You have been made monkeys of by a couple of Spanish spies. Got that? You have botched up the whole scheme. Got that? You have ruined us all."

"But—but——" began Pierre, but Lacroix snarled at him and he stopped.

"We'd better get away," said Beppi, and his eyes went from side to side. "Give us some money and we'll scatter."

"Give you some money!" said Lacroix with a cracked laugh. "Give you——"

"Certainly," said Beppi firmly. "We have even spent our own

money on this brilliant scheme of yours and I have only two thousand francs left."

"I too am out of funds," said Pierre. "I have only four thousand left, and Le Poisson here is cleaned out. He paid for the——"

"I have none at all," said Lacroix. "The police pounced on me at that hotel at Arnage and I did not even take my hat. I left in a car which—— That doesn't matter. I went back to try to get in, but the police were searching the place; they will have found it all by now. It is I that must have money, you will——"

"One understands," said the inarticulate one slowly. "It was, after all, the *patron* who shot the Englishman and that other. If he is caught it will be serious for him."

His companions looked at him with the usual astonishment, as though a waxwork had spoken; when they looked back at Lacroix he had a gun in his hand.

"Your wallets on the table, please. Do as I tell you, you know I can shoot."

Beppi slowly drew out his wallet and laid it on the table.

"Pierre," said Lacroix sharply, and Pierre also unwillingly obeyed. Lacroix, still holding his gun, gathered up the two wallets with his other hand and dropped them in his pocket.

"You others——" he began, but the man called Le Poisson, moved beyond himself, uttered a yell of rage, drew a small pistol from his pocket, and fired it in the general direction of Lacroix. The bullet hit the face of a clock over Lacroix's head and the broken glass fell upon his head and shoulders. Perhaps this disturbed his aim, for when he fired in reply Beppi uttered a yell and fell to the floor. Forgan and Campbell were there already, in a corner behind a table.

Instantly the group broke up. The three still active members of the escort made a rush for the door at the back; they tore it open and leapt out. The open door disclosed a small yard; even as the fugitives entered it they were seized upon and overpowered by four capable men in a variety of plain clothes. One was to all appearances a baker's roundsman, for he carried a basket containing loaves which must have been stale since they had not been changed for four days. Another carried the broom of a street sweeper. Whatever their dress, they had not been far away from the group for nearly a week; Forgan and Campbell had found their attendance an enormous moral support. There was a certain amount of outcry attending the arrests, and the two Englishmen nudged each other.

Lacroix looked once into the yard and immediately ran down the café towards the front entrance. Since he was still carrying a gun in his hand, the proprietor and his waiter made no uncivil attempt to detain him. They did not even remind him that he had not paid. He wriggled through the broken panel of the door and disappeared in the crowd.

Forgan got up and courteously helped Campbell to disentangle himself from the legs of a chair with which he had become involved. Beppi was still rolling on the floor with his head streaked with blood and appealing in impassioned tones to as many saints as he could remember after many years of moral absence. He appeared to be of Italian origin.

Two of the men came in from the yard, grinning cheerfully and asking if this was the other one. They picked him up, shook him, told him it was only a nick out of one of his ears which stuck out too much anyway, and removed him, still bleating.

Campbell made a rush for the proprietor's telephone and rang up Letord at the Quai des Orfèvres.

CHAPTER 19 *On the Tiles*

LACROIX, otherwise Tiffet, dodged in and out among the crowd, pocketing his gun as he went, since it was no part of his design to appear in any way noticeable. He passed through warring shareholders and indignant Poujadists until he came near one end of the long narrow battle. He was for a moment penned in; something caught his eye and he glanced up to see what looked like the grandfather of all bombs descending upon him; since, on account of the press, he could neither move nor lift his hands, the object struck him upon the head and immediately burst.

It took him a moment to realize that that which streamed stickily over his face and shoulders was not his own brains; the next moment his nose informed him that it was melon—very overripe, but still melon. He turned and made his way blindly, scraping and pawing at his face as he went, past the café again and along the road to the other end of the conflict. Here, in a quiet doorway, he wiped pips and melon juice out of his eyes and looked about him. There, just in front of him, was a large limousine; empty, facing away from the conflict.

The young and intelligent chauffeur who had been in charge of that car had succeeded in finding his master, still recognizable in spite of having lost his hat, his watch, and one sleeve of his coat. He had acquired in exchange a sore ear, some mud in his hair, and a hack on the ankle. Master and chauffeur struggled along together, with the chauffeur offering encouragement.

"Lean on me, monsieur. Ah, *les crapauds!* Not much further. There is the car now. Another twenty metres only——"

But when it was another ten metres only, the big limousine glided silently away and left them standing.

Hambledon and Letord were together at the Sûreté.

"They say," said Letord, "that it is impossible to keep the news back any longer. They will publish tomorrow morning."

"Let them," said Hambledon. "We know who the leader of that gang is. Lacroix, of course, do you not agree? You will catch him if you look in the right place quickly enough."

Letord nodded. "Also, when we rope in his assistants—and we can do that at any time—they will talk, believe me. Those types, loyalty is not in their alphabet. Besides, they will have me to deal with. I will have them in here and they will tell Papa all their little secrets."

"If they know any," said Hambledon. "Those two who abducted Dupont were not very helpful."

Letord shrugged that off.

"He was in a very nice position—Lacroix, I mean—at Arnage-sur-Loire. It seems that the hotel was his own and it was quite prosperous itself, was it not? Yes. Lacroix had those room telephones put in as an improvement when he took over; it was an ideal arrangement. The gang were summoned there by letter and told to be in the bedroom of one of them at a certain hour to receive instructions over the telephone; they had no means of knowing which room the voice spoke from, nor who spoke. It might have been another hotel guest merely there for the day. Nor did it matter which rooms they had, Lacroix need take no interest in the allocations. He need only look up the number on a——" The telephone rang. "Excuse me. What? . . . Turn out the riot squad in two sections, let them enter the street from either end and clear up as they go. What? . . . I am not interested in politics. When they are brought in I will talk politics to them myself. Warn the fire brigade for action; hoses may be useful." Letord replaced the receiver. "There is a riot outside the offices of the Franco-Camposian Company, but I do not gather that your scoundrels are responsible this time. The Franco-Camposian shareholders are fighting the Poujadists, it seems."

"For heaven's sake, why?"

"On a matter of principle, they say."

Hambledon was reasonably familiar with French mental processes, but this left him speechless. However, a moment or two later the telephone rang again and this time it was Campbell;

Letord motioned to Hambledon to take up the extension receiver.

They both listened in silence to the rapid account of what had just taken place.

"He identified himself as *le patron* by producing three dried beans," added Campbell. "You remember, Power had some in that little silver box. Skewbald beans. The others had 'em too."

"You say he took their wallets," said Hambledon. "How much money, do you know?"

"Six thousand francs altogether. He has also a five-chambered revolver shy one shot."

When Letord had all the information Campbell could give him, he rang off and looked across the desk at Hambledon.

"That eel in human form——" he began, but Tommy cut him short.

"Six thousand francs is not what Lacroix would call money. He must have some to get away. I am going down to the Café de Bruges, just in case. You have a man there?"

"Cardeur, you know him. Plain clothes. Madame will no doubt be delighted to see you."

Hambledon scorned to answer. He walked up to the Café de Bruges and found the plain-clothes detective Cardeur looking at a display of paper-backed novels in a stationer's window.

"You have not seen Lacroix?"

"No, monsieur. No one at all of that description has entered the café."

"Whom have you got watching the back entrance?"

The detective looked surprised. "But, monsieur, there is no other entrance unless one is prepared to scale the walls of back yards."

Hambledon thought that that was not very difficult if there were one or two convenient dustbins to stand on, but he did not say so.

"I think you had better stay outside here unless you see him turn in. If you do, follow him in."

"Very good, monsieur."

Hambledon went into the café, which was completely empty except for the old waiter, who was doddering about with a duster, tidying up and setting chairs straight.

"What? You have the whole place to yourself alone?"

The old man smiled. "As is usual at this hour, monsieur. A little later, in half an hour's time, the clients will begin to come."

"And Madame?"

"Upstairs. At this hour it is her custom to rest."

"Let us not disturb her, I will wait a little while."

"Monsieur is always welcome. Would Monsieur care to take a little glass of something?"

Hambledon ordered cognac; the old waiter served him and then went on with his duties. Tommy sipped the brandy and, waiting till the man's back was turned, took out his gun and checked over it. That he should do this during the course of the day was very unusual for him; normally the gun was checked over when he first picked it up, and Hambledon was not of a fidgeting habit. The fact was that he was uneasy, and growing more so every minute. There was something wrong with the place. "If I were a dog," he thought, "my hackles would be standing up. There's danger here somewhere. I think Lacroix is not far off."

He turned and spoke to the waiter. "Tell me, did you know Madame's husband at all? Monsieur Tiffet?"

"Oh no, monsieur. He was dead before I came here to work."

"I see, yes. Have you been in here all the afternoon—for the past hour, at least?"

"But yes, monsieur. That is, in and out. Madame's sister, in the kitchen, I help her a little when there is time."

So Lacroix could have slipped in by the back door if he had watched his moment. Hambledon's fingers tapped a soundless tattoo on the bar, and everything was horribly quiet, as though the house were holding its breath. Quite suddenly, from just overhead, a door slammed and there was a muffled thump as though somebody or something had fallen down. Hambledon set down his glass and the old waiter stood still, looking up.

"Where did that noise come from?"

"Madame's room is directly overhead."

They heard a noise like a door being kicked, and at once there followed a loud scream and a cry for help in a woman's voice. Hambledon, with his hand on the gun in his pocket, rushed up the stairs, with the old man close upon his heels. Even as they ran there came the sound of a shot and more screams.

They burst into Madame's room and found her lying on the

floor in front of an inner door. She had been bound to a chair and gagged but had managed to slip the gag off.

"My husband—he tried to kill me——"

"Where is he now?" demanded Hambledon.

"In there—he cannot get out; the catch, it is from the outside only. He is hunting for my money, I would not tell him—he went in there and I threw myself against the door——"

Hambledon hauled her out of the way without ceremony and told the waiter to look after her. The door was a flimsy affair with a bullethole through it. "Three shots left," thought Hambledon, and then bellowed: "Lacroix!"

There was no answer but the sounds of movement and then a sharp thud.

"That," sobbed Madame, who was working up for an attack of hysterics, "is the trap door."

"Hell!" exploded Hambledon. "Where does that lead to?"

"Only the loft—and the roof—oh, oh!"

Hambledon stood back against the doorpost, flung the door open, and awaited reprisals. None came, so he looked into the inner room. There were a few chairs needing repair, a table with a broken leg, a horizontal ladder against one wall leading to a loft above, and that was all. Hambledon paused; to open that trap door in the face of a man with a gun would be not only suicide but silly. The one window was barred and looked down upon the street.

Footsteps overhead, stamping about in one place, then a rending sound as of splintering wood and a slithering noise. Something fell past the window to break, with an astonishingly loud crash, in the street below. Hambledon flung up the window and excoriated his face against the rusty bars in time to see the detective Cardeur run across from a shop door opposite and disappear directly beneath him.

"Gone to ring up the riot squad," said Hambledon, and he was quite right, except that Cardeur first rang the fire brigade and told them to send an escape to the Café de Bruges, Rue de l'Arbre Vert, vite, vite!

The wreckage in the street consisted of broken glass and pieces of wooden framing.

"Madame! Is there a window in the loft?"

The old waiter answered. "A skylight only, monsieur."

Hambledon swore under his breath, for the prospect of chasing an armed man over the roof tops of Paris he found quite repellent. But if he did not follow, the fellow might escape again. He climbed up the ladder and lifted the trap an inch or two. Nothing happened except that air blew in, and there were scraping, sliding noises above, followed by the clatter of falling tiles. Lacroix was on the roof.

Hambledon went up in the loft, which had no ceiling; the beams and rafters which carried the roof were exposed and it was evident that the roof rose sharply at front and back to a lengthwise ridge in the middle. There was one chimney stack near the skylight, now a gaping hole in the front slope, and another further along on the backward slope. Lacroix could be heard making his way towards the further chimney stack.

"I suppose there's a way down from that end," said Hambledon resignedly. "Well, here goes," and he climbed out of the hole to emerge upon the roof.

In point of fact, there had been another building next door with a roof at the same level and another skylight like the first. It was not until Lacroix had crawled, flat on his stomach, to the low wall which had divided the roofs that he found the house next door was in process of being pulled down and was now thirty feet below him and jagged at that. He turned carefully just in time to see the disappearing shoes of some man who had followed him out of the skylight and was now sheltering behind the first chimney stack.

Lacroix slid down his side of the roof to come to rest against the second, and his haste sent a cascade of tiles slithering into the yard behind. But he was also behind the ridge of the roof, and when his opponent put his head over it—— He drew his revolver and waited.

Hambledon looked down once and wished he had not. There did not appear to be a gutter at the edge of the roof; there might be one below the edge, out of sight; if there was, it was probably rotten. The thing to do was to draw those three shots. Lacroix was an excellent shot with a rifle but probably not so good with a revolver; it was very seldom that a man was equally good with both weapons. Of course that was why he had borrowed Barbeau's rifle to shoot Power. Hambledon's jaw came forward, and he left his own gun where it was, in his pocket. The man who shot Power was going to be taken alive and handed over to the police alive, and the guillotine could have him.

Hambledon loosened some tiles from their supporting battens to get a toe hold between them; with Madame Tiffet's roof three or four descending tiles involved a dozen or more in their fall. Crashing sounds below in the street were followed by suitable cries. An intelligent interest was being taken—good.

Hambledon put his head over the ridge of the roof and ducked again, and a bullet smacked into the chimney pot a yard above his head. Wild shooting. One less.

He moved along till he was above the skylight and tried again; this time the bullet sang over his head and he felt the wind of it in his hair. Not such wild shooting, but only one left. If Lacroix could be persuaded to think that his final shot was successful, perhaps he would come within reach——

Hambledon returned to the chimney stack, arranged a safe hold for his hands, and ventured a third time. Lacroix obliged with a final shot which actually nicked the edge of the brickwork before it ricocheted off into oblivion, but this shot was followed by a strangled yelp and a lot of kicking which sent more tiles after their fellows. Then there was silence.

Presently Lacroix made a move; he could be heard to be clambering along the roof. Hambledon, looking as dead as possible against his chimney, saw the movement from the tail of his eye and waited. Lacroix paused, apparently thought him beyond harm, and made to pass him by——

Hambledon exploded into action, seized Lacroix by one wrist and his throat, and proceeded to choke him into insensibility, but Lacroix resisted violently and there was a struggle which ended in both men rolling down the roof. Lacroix clung desperately to the bottom edge of the skylight with both hands. Hambledon's feet went over the edge and found the gutter, which promptly broke away. He felt himself sliding and there were no missing tiles there to offer him handhold.

"This," he said to himself, "is it," and frantically flung out his hands for something to hold him; he found one of Lacroix's ankles and froze on to it with both hands, still slipping. The ankle came with him as he slid slowly over the edge and hung clear above the street.

"Let go!" gasped Lacroix.

"Never," said Tommy grimly, and a phrase came to his mind about "a grip which even death could not loosen." How unpleasant, to have to be buried with Lacroix because nobody could part them.

"I implore Monsieur to let go," said Lacroix in a tone of entreaty, and at that moment there rose to their ears the sound of the horn which is reserved for the use of official vehicles in most continental countries. "Hoo-hah! Hoo-hah!"

"The police," said Lacroix.

"No. Hold on, Lacroix. The fire escape. Hold on."

The escape wheeled into position, winding up its ladder as it did so.

"Hold on, Lacroix——"

"*Merde!*" yelled Lacroix suddenly. "Get away! I'm being poked off with a broom—stop it——"

Hambledon felt under his feet the top rungs of the escape ladder being manoeuvred between him and the wall. It took his weight, and Lacroix at once began to struggle.

"No, you don't," said Hambledon between his teeth and hung on grimly. In the open square of the skylight appeared the face of the old waiter with his white hair standing on end and a broom in his hand.

"Monsieur," he quavered, addressing Hambledon, "monsieur, shall I smite him?"

Someone's arm came round Hambledon's legs, someone came up beside him on the ladder; it was the detective Cardeur. There was a rattle and two loud clicks by Hambledon's ear.

"Let Monsieur descend," said Cardeur. "That one cannot escape. I have handcuffed his ankle to the top rung of the ladder. Then, if he gives any more trouble we can just wind him down a little and convey him to the Sûreté like a monkey on a stick. Let Monsieur take his time, there is no hurry now."

It did take Hambledon some time to reach the ground, for reaction was upon him and his legs felt like boiled macaroni; when he stepped off at the bottom he staggered and someone caught his arm.

"Why the devil," demanded Letord, "didn't you shoot him instead of risking your life like that?"

"Madame," explained Hambledon a little breathlessly. "You can make her a widow when I am safely out of reach."